BENJAMIN FRANKLINSTEIN
MEETS
THOMAS DEADISON

BENJAMIN FRANKLINSTEIN
MEETS
THOMAS DEADISON

Wherein is contained
an Accounting of the Quest by our Subject
and his Young Companions to subdue an Army of Hypnotized
Zombies and thwart the Evil Plans of the Emperor

By MATTHEW McELLIGOTT
& LARRY TUXBURY. Philom.

Illustrated by Matthew McElligott
Printed and fold by G. P. Putnam's Sons
An Imprint of Penguin Group (USA) Inc.
At the New Printing Office near the Market.

G. P. PUTNAM'S SONS • A DIVISION OF PENGUIN YOUNG READERS GROUP.
Published by The Penguin Group.
Penguin Group (USA) Inc., 375 Hudson Street, New York, NY 10014, U.S.A.
Penguin Group (Canada), 90 Eglinton Avenue East, Suite 700, Toronto, Ontario M4P 2Y3,
Canada (a division of Pearson Penguin Canada Inc.).
Penguin Books Ltd, 80 Strand, London WC2R 0RL, England.
Penguin Ireland, 25 St. Stephen's Green, Dublin 2, Ireland
(a division of Penguin Books Ltd).
Penguin Group (Australia), 250 Camberwell Road, Camberwell, Victoria 3124,
Australia (a division of Pearson Australia Group Pty Ltd).
Penguin Books India Pvt Ltd, 11 Community Centre, Panchsheel Park,
New Delhi—110 017, India.
Penguin Group (NZ), 67 Apollo Drive, Rosedale, Auckland 0632, New Zealand
(a division of Pearson New Zealand Ltd).
Penguin Books (South Africa) (Pty) Ltd, 24 Sturdee Avenue, Rosebank,
Johannesburg 2196, South Africa.
Penguin Books Ltd, Registered Offices: 80 Strand, London WC2R 0RL, England.

Published simultaneously in Canada. Printed in the United States of America.
Design by Marikka Tamura and Annie Ericsson. Text set in ITC Cheltenham.
The art was done in a combination of traditional and digital techniques.
Library of Congress Cataloging-in-Publication Data
McElligott, Matthew. Benjamin Franklinstein meets Thomas Deadison /
Matthew McElligott, Larry David Tuxbury ; illustrated by Matthew McElligott.
p. cm.—(Benjamin Franklinstein ; 3) Summary: "Ben and Victor must stop a mysterious
lightbulb company from brainwashing Philadelphia"—Provided by publisher.
1. Franklin, Benjamin, 1706–1790—Juvenile fiction. 2. Edison, Thomas A. (Thomas Alva),
1847–1931—Juvenile fiction. [1. Franklin, Benjamin, 1706–1790—Fiction. 2. Edison,
Thomas A. (Thomas Alva), 1847–1931. 3. Scientists—Fiction. 4. Secret societies—Fiction.]
I. Tuxbury, Larry. II. Title.
PZ7.M478448Bt 2012 [Fic]—dc23 2012001615
ISBN 978-0-399-25481-9
1 3 5 7 9 10 8 6 4 2

For Christy and Anthony.
Also—Larry, you are feeling very sleepy. Your eyelids
are growing heavy. Matt is great. Matt is great . . .
—M.M.

For Melanie, Nina, and Ella.
Matt is great.
—L.T.

Take Courage, Mortal;
Death can't banish thee
out of the Universe.

—Benjamin Franklin

FREQUENTLY ASKED QUESTIONS
about Benjamin Franklinstein

Is Benjamin Franklin still alive?

Yes.

How is that possible?

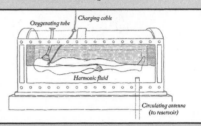

Centuries ago, Franklin and a group of scientists called the Modern Order of Prometheus invented the Leyden casket. This device allowed Franklin to "sleep" for centuries in a state of suspended animation.

What was the mission of the Modern Order of Prometheus?

To preserve the world's greatest inventors, then awaken them when society faced a Great Emergency.

Was Franklin the only inventor preserved by the Order?

No, there were others. For example, Orville and Wilbur Wright, inventors of the airplane, were also preserved.

Does the Modern Order of Prometheus still exist?

Yes, but the organization is in trouble. A mysterious figure known as the Emperor is attempting to control it. A small handful of scientists—the Promethean Underground—is trying to discover who the Emperor is and stop him.

Where was Franklin preserved?

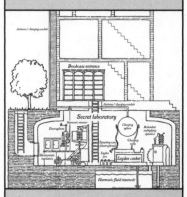

In a secret basement laboratory beneath a house in Philadelphia. This house is currently owned by Mary Godwin and her son, Victor. Franklin rents the downstairs apartment.

Other than members of the Order, who knows that Franklin and the Wright brothers are alive?

Victor Godwin; his best friend, Scott Weaver; and Scott's dad, Skip.

Who is the Emperor?

Napoléon Bonaparte, former emperor of France and one of the greatest military generals who ever lived.

Didn't he die hundreds of years ago?

Apparently not . . .

PROLOGUE
Philadelphia, 1821

The Emperor sat alone in a blackened room. He did his best thinking in darkness.

He had hoped to create a better world. A perfect world. But when the leaders of other *lesser* countries rejected his brilliant ideas, he had no choice but to go to war. If they would not accept his plan, he would force it upon them. It would be a new world—a greater world!

At first his army and navy had triumphed. They had begun to create a glorious empire! But then he faced horrible defeat in Russia and finally at Waterloo. And then he had been imprisoned on the island of St. Helena.

His jailers expected him to die there.

That was then. Now he had a greater plan.

The door creaked open and a lantern illuminated the basement laboratory.

"Empereur Napoléon?" a voice inquired. *"C'est moi, votre subordonné, Moreau."*

"Speak English, Moreau!" the man spat. "We are no longer in France. Here in Philadelphia, no one must know where you are truly from."

Moreau placed the lantern on a table. He pulled a lever, and the room slowly filled with a soft blue light.

"Forgive me," he begged, struggling to conceal his accent. "It is almost time for your long sleep."

Napoléon arose from his throne. "Excellent. Have you given the others their orders?"

"Absolutely, my Emperor."

"Repeat them back to me."

Moreau's mouth went dry. He swallowed. "I instructed Chevalier, Fournier, and Lefevre to find a perfect double for you. They will sail to the isle of St. Helena and place him into your bed. The world will soon believe that you, the great Napoléon Bonaparte, are dead."

A thin smile grew on Napoléon's face. "Very good. And then?"

"They shall arrive here by next week. As you sleep in the Leyden casket, we shall secretly begin taking control of the Modern Order of Prometheus, following your instructions to the letter."

"Then all is ready."

Napoléon mounted the steps to the Leyden casket. Cast in iron, silver, and gold by French artisans, it looked like an ornate bathtub. Intricate carvings of battle horses, cannons, and an eagle wearing a crown decorated its sides. It was supported by four gilded legs with sculpted lions' feet at the bottom. A casket built for a king!

He climbed into the glowing harmonic fluid that would preserve him for centuries to come.

"Wait!" Moreau said. "I am uncertain about one thing."

"Uncertain?" Napoléon asked, raising an eyebrow.

"I have read Dr. Franklin's secret journals, Excellency," Moreau stammered. "He feared that this process might be dangerous. If awakened too often—for example, every ten years, as you have planned—you could risk physical damage."

Napoléon considered Moreau's words. The plan was perfect, wasn't it? Every ten years, he would be revived to reassert his control over the Order. Then one grand day, he would awaken all the inventors to join his army and create a greater world. The future would be his.

It was worth the risk.

"Dr. Franklin's suggestion was merely a theory," Napoléon said. "Besides, I am no ordinary man. I am Napoléon Bonaparte, Future Emperor of the World. My brilliance shall not be dimmed."

"But Excellency—"

"Enough!" He glared at Moreau. "How many times have I told you? *Conquest is risk!*"

With that, the Emperor placed the airtight breathing mask over his mouth and nose. He slipped into his casket, fell into a deep sleep, and began dreaming of the future.

NAPOLÉON'S TO-DO LIST

☑ *Create plan to take over Modern Order of Prometheus.*

☑ *Send Agent Moreau to Philadelphia to prepare for my arrival.*

☑ *Fake own death and escape from St. Helena Island.*

☑ *Set sail for America.*

☐ *Begin suspended animation in Leyden casket.*

☐ *Awaken every ten years and take over more of the Order, preserve more inventors.*

☐ *When time is right, awaken Benjamin Franklin. Take control of him and all other inventors.*

☐ *Use inventors to take over the world.*

CHAPTER ONE
Near Philadelphia, Modern Day

Victor Godwin clenched the frame of the flying machine and tried to focus on the sky above. He knew there was absolutely no reason to be afraid. He just had to look at things rationally. The gyroplane was perfectly safe, and he was strapped in tight. Plus, the pilot was a pro. After all, the man had practically invented flying.

"Everything okay back there?" said Orville Wright.

"Yup."

Benjamin Franklin looked back from the copilot's seat. "Are you certain, Victor?"

"Yup."

One-word answers, Victor thought. That was the key. Keep it short. Especially since he'd forgotten to pack a barf bag.

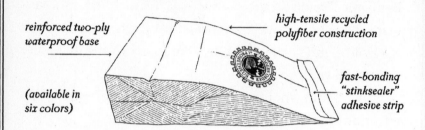

reinforced two-ply
waterproof base

high-tensile recycled
polyfiber construction

(available in
six colors)

fast-bonding
"stinksealer"
adhesive strip

The Promethean gyroplane was a new invention: part helicopter, part Wright brothers airplane, and part Franklin kite. Victor had been given the honor of coming along on today's test flight. So far, the gyroplane was working perfectly.

All Victor had to do was hang on for a few more minutes. Soon he'd be back on solid ground at the Promethean testing area.

Orville looked back over his shoulder. "What say we take her in a little closer?" He pushed forward on a stick, and the gyroplane dipped downward. Victor felt his stomach rise up into his chest.

He knew he should be relishing every second of the experience. How many people in history had ever had the chance to fly with one of the Wright brothers? It was the opportunity of a lifetime.

He couldn't wait for it to be over.

Victor liked order. He liked plans. He liked knowing

exactly what was going to happen next. But ever since Benjamin Franklin had moved into the downstairs apartment, his whole world had turned upside down.

"Hold tight!" called Orville. "I'm going to try flying her upside down."

"No!" Victor shouted. "I mean . . . maybe you should wait until the next test flight."

Orville laughed. "Just kidding! I'm going to circle around a couple more times, then bring it in for a landing. Okay with you?"

"Yup."

The gyroplane leveled off, and Victor relaxed his grip on the frame. He glanced down and watched the ground pass beneath him. Now that he knew the flight was almost over, he had to admit that he was enjoying it. A little.

He let out a sigh of relief.

BOOM!!!

There was a bright flash behind him. The gyroplane shook and began to nose-dive.

"What was that?" Orville yelled, trying to regain control. The harmonic fluid coursing through his veins allowed him to move at superhuman speed. He began pulling levers and flipping switches, his hands a blur.

"Something exploded!" Victor shouted. "The tail's on fire!"

A long trail of black smoke streamed out behind the gyroplane. Flames ate away at the tail, inching toward Victor.

Franklin looked back in alarm.

"Grab the fire extinguisher at your feet, Dr. Franklin," ordered Orville. "Victor, release your seat belt and join us up here!"

Victor fumbled with his belt and unbuckled the clasp. The plane shuddered and rocked from side to side as Orville struggled to keep it steady. Victor clutched the seats for support. Behind him, the flames drew nearer.

Up ahead, he could see the pond at the edge of the Promethean testing area, and just beyond it, the landing strip.

"Hold tight for just a minute more," said Orville. "We're almost there!"

BOOM!!!

A second explosion rocked the plane, and it tipped violently to the left.

Victor lost his grip on the seats and tumbled out over the side. In desperation, he reached out into the empty air. His hands caught a metal wing strut. He hung there, dangling in the sky, as the plane began to spiral down.

"Help!"

"Victor, we can't level off with you out there," Orville said. "We're nearly over the pond. You'll have to jump and swim to shore. It's our only hope!"

"But—"

"Have no fear, Victor," Franklin said. "You can do it!"

"But Ben, I—"

With a thunderous boom, the gyroplane jolted and

hacked out another cloud of black smoke. Victor's fingers slipped free. He fell.

"But I can't swim!"

THE PROMETHEAN GYROPLANE

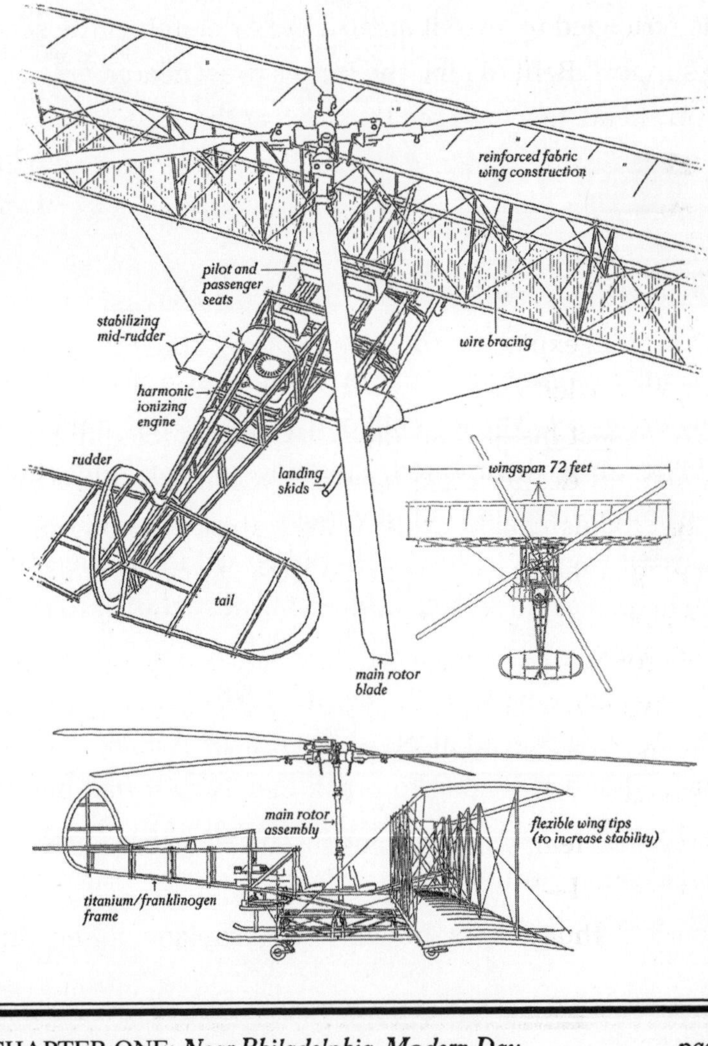

reinforced fabric
wing construction

pilot and
passenger
seats

stabilizing
mid-rudder

wire bracing

harmonic
ionizing
engine

rudder

landing
skids

wingspan 72 feet

tail

main rotor
blade

main rotor
assembly

flexible wing tips
(to increase stability)

titanium/franklinogen
frame

CHAPTER TWO
A Daring Rescue

Everything happened in a fraction of a second. The sting of impact. The icy chill of the water. Then darkness.

Victor was disoriented, spinning. A dim light shone from somewhere just out of view.

Focus! He had to focus. He pulled wildly at the water with his arms and kicked hard, trying desperately to reach the surface.

Was he even moving? He couldn't tell.

Something tugged at his shirt. A fish? A snake? Victor thrashed and struggled to break free. Now it had him by the shoulder, pulling him deeper. He felt himself weakening. His lungs burned.

He was going to die.

Then suddenly there was bright light everywhere. Cool air rushed into his lungs. Victor choked and sputtered, bobbing in the gentle waves of the pond as a firm grip held him afloat.

"Ben!"

"Relax, Victor. Slow, deep breaths. You'll be fine." Franklin gestured across the pond. "As will Orville, I see."

Two hundred yards away, the gyroplane bounced and skidded onto a long field of grass, a ribbon of thick black smoke trailing behind. Dr. Gwynn, a Promethean engineer, rushed to its side.

"Try to float on your back. I'll take it from here." Franklin swung his arm tight across Victor's chest and began to tow him toward shore with a steady sidestroke. "I was quite a swimmer in my day. Perhaps you've heard of swim fins?"

Victor nodded.

"My invention! I wore them on my hands, but I've noticed that today the fashion is to put them on the feet. To each his own, I suppose."

Even without flippers, Franklin was a strong swimmer. As he pushed on, Victor did his best to focus on the sky above. Within just a few minutes they were at the dock, where a familiar hand was waiting to help him up.

"That was *so cool*! Best cannonball ever! And you should have seen Ben dive out of the plane after you. *Wow!*"

Victor winced. Only Scott Weaver could find something

like this entertaining. Didn't he realize Victor had nearly died?

Victor took Scott's hand and climbed onto the dock.

Dr. Gwynn ran over with a towel. "Are you all right, Victor?"

"I'm fine. Just a little shaken up." He gathered the towel close and tried to catch his breath. "How's Orville?"

"He's fine, but this particular gyroplane is ruined. Right now, he and Wilbur are trying to figure out what went wrong."

"He's an amazing pilot," said Victor. "If it hadn't been for him and Ben, I—Hey, where *is* Ben?"

"Over there with Jaime and the others," said Scott.

At the edge of the shore, Franklin lay on his back, his legs twitching. Two Promethean scientists huddled over him.

"Something's wrong," said Victor. "Sparks are coming out of his neck bolts."

"Is that bad?" asked Scott.

"Very."

There was a flash, like someone taking a picture, then a puff of smoke. Franklin's leg stopped moving, and he was completely still.

"Quick!" one of the scientists ordered. "Take him inside!"

To an outside observer, the Promethean testing area looked like any private camp. There were woods, fields, a

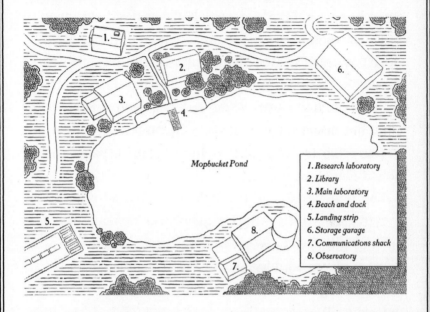

Mopbucket Pond

1. Research laboratory
2. Library
3. Main laboratory
4. Beach and dock
5. Landing strip
6. Storage garage
7. Communications shack
8. Observatory

dock, a beach, and several cabinlike buildings. But inside those buildings, the scientists of the Promethean Underground carried out some of the most advanced research in the world.

Right now, that research was focused entirely on one man.

In the basement of Building Three, Benjamin Franklin's body was stretched out on a long metal table. Cables ran from the bolts in his neck to a rack of computers, where doctors and engineers monitored his vital signs.

"Is he dead?" whispered Scott.

"No," said Victor, "but it's serious. The pond water must have shorted out his battery belt. It was never designed to go underwater."

Victor had invented the battery belt to help fix one of Franklin's biggest problems: The old man was constantly running out of power. When he had been preserved in 1790, harmonic technology was brand-new. It would not be perfected until the time of the Wright brothers, over a century later.

The first version of the belt had been a series of rechargeable batteries that Franklin wore beneath his coat. But recently, Promethean scientists had replaced it with a more advanced, high-power lithium polymer matrix. It worked amazingly well—provided Franklin stayed out of the water.

"Any updates?"

"Oh—hi, Jaime," said Victor, startled. Jaime Winters had an unsettling habit of appearing out of nowhere. "No, nothing yet, from what I can tell. He's stable, but . . . well, he still hasn't moved."

"He's like a statue," said Scott. "From a museum."

Jaime snorted. "Thanks for the clarification, Scott."

"No problem. Say, can I ask you something? How come you wear those sunglasses all the time, even indoors?"

"How come you ask annoying questions all the time?"

Scott shrugged. "It's just what I do."

"Well, wearing sunglasses is what *I* do."

Victor winced. Jaime Winters had a habit of taking out her stress on the easiest target in the room, and that target was usually Scott. Fortunately, Scott never seemed to notice.

To be fair, Jaime had a lot to be stressed about. Her parents had been Custodians in the Modern Order of Prometheus. But they, and many others, had disappeared months ago in the Emperor's latest maneuver to gain control of the Order. Since then, Jaime had devoted herself to helping the Promethean Underground fight back. Although she was roughly Victor and Scott's age, she had to spend her days acting like an adult. It had to be hard, Victor thought.

"There's not much we can do here," said Victor. "How about we get some air?"

Jaime nodded. "I meant to tell you—Orville and Wilbur are waiting at the field to say good-bye."

"I'll meet you there," said Victor. "Where's the bathroom?"

At the men's room, Victor held the door as a janitor shoved past him with a ladder and a box of lightbulbs. His hands were still shaking from the morning's excitement, and his stomach had terrible cramps. He entered a stall and sat down.

He had tried to hide it around Jaime and Scott, but he was deeply concerned about Ben. Victor had dropped his phone in a puddle once, and the damage to its electronics had been instant and beyond repair. Franklin's own electrical system was not all that different. A short circuit to

his battery matrix could have easily—

. . . listen . . .

Victor looked around.

"Hello?" said Victor. "Is someone there?"

Silence.

He ducked down and peered beneath the stall. No feet. He was still alone in the bathroom.

Weird. He was sure he had heard a voice. But stress could do that to a person.

Victor finished up and raced out to join the others.

At the end of the field, Victor found Scott examining the remains of the gyroplane with his dad, Skip Weaver. Jaime took photos of the wreck, while Orville and Wilbur worked at superspeed to analyze the damage and make repairs.

"Mr. Weaver!" said Victor. "We didn't expect to see you so early. Is everything all right?"

"Sure is," said Skip. "But it sounds like you had quite a scare. How are you doing?"

"Better," said Victor.

"Glad to hear it," said Skip. "We've got a slight change of plans. Mrs. Weaver has one of her fund-raisers at the Arthur Parker Art Park tonight. Scott and I have to—I mean *get* to—be there. I'm afraid I'm going to have to take you guys home a little early."

"When you're there, be sure to visit *The Emperor's*

Spaghetti," said Orville. "It's our favorite sculpture."

"Will do," Skip said, laughing.

"So what do you guys think happened to your plane?" asked Victor.

Wilbur frowned. "We don't know. There's nothing flammable in the tail. There's no reason it should have exploded."

"I can think of one reason," said Jaime. "Sabotage."

"Sabotage?" Victor said. "You think someone here is trying to destroy the gyroplane?"

"And maybe kill a couple of important inventors at the same time," Jaime said, looking at Orville.

"We're going to keep both of our gyroplanes grounded until we know for sure," said Wilbur. "With luck, we'll be ready to resume sky patrols by the end of the week."

"Plus, back at the shop we still have several hundred bicycles to rebuild and return to our customers," added Orville. "It's going to be a busy week."

"For us too," added Scott mournfully. "School starts tomorrow."

MEANWHILE . . .

A tired-looking man sat slumped behind a messy desk at the Philadelphia Department of Streets. The fluorescent ceiling lights reflected dully off his head.

"I'm sorry, Mr. Thomason," he said, "but the Street Lighting Unit is responsible for one hundred thousand streetlights and eighteen thousand alley lights. We don't have the money for that much new lighting, even your Infinity Bulbs. Maybe next year."

Ed Thomason stood in front of the desk, straightening his bow tie. "I don't think you fully grasp the brilliance of my invention, Mr. Swan. If you replace all the city's streetlamps with Infinity Bulbs, Philadelphia will save millions in electricity bills. They use only a fraction of the energy your current lights do."

Mr. Swan shook his head. "I wish I could help you, but it's just not going to happen this year."

"But Mr. Swan, if you bent the rules—took a few shortcuts, perhaps—you *could* move this process along, couldn't you?"

Mr. Swan sat up straight in his chair. His face reddened. "I don't break the rules for anybody, Mr. Thomason. Now get out of my office."

"I think you misunderstand me," Mr. Thomason said. "Please give me one last chance. I'd like to show you something."

He took the reading lamp off Mr. Swan's desk and unscrewed the bulb. "Watch closely."

Mr. Thomason dropped the lightbulb into the wastebasket and stuck his finger into the lamp's socket.

"Hey!" Mr. Swan shouted. "Are you crazy? You'll be—"

But he never finished his sentence.

Mr. Thomason's entire body began to glow from within. First a soft orange, and then a bright white. He shone like a human lightbulb filament. His glow pulsated, throbbing like a heartbeat.

Mr. Swan tried to speak, tried to move, but could do neither.

"You will follow my command."

The voice seemed to come from everywhere.

"I will," Mr. Swan droned.

"You will replace all city streetlights with Infinity Bulbs."

"Yes."

"This is a good decision."

"It is."

"It will save the city money and electricity. This is the right thing to do."

"This is the right thing to do."

"You will begin now."

Mr. Swan awoke at his desk and blinked his eyes.

"I must have fallen asleep," he muttered to himself. "I'm overworked."

He looked at the newly signed contracts in front of him. *Ah, yes,* he thought. *The Infinity Unlimited streetlight contract. This is a good decision. This is the right thing to do. I will begin now.*

He picked up the phone and made a call.

CHAPTER THREE

Back to School

It felt strange to walk in to the first day of school so unprepared.

In the past, Victor would have started getting ready weeks in advance. He would have memorized his locker combination, color-coded his folders, mapped out his class locations, and calculated his travel time between each point. And he wouldn't have missed the bus. But this year, those things didn't seem quite so important.

At least Ben was doing better. Jaime had texted Victor that morning. Dr. Gwynn had moved Franklin from the testing area to Promethean Underground Headquarters. Franklin was up and about, and a small team of scientists was working on a more reliable battery belt. Victor wanted to visit, but Jaime insisted that the location of headquarters had to remain secret, even to him. After all, the Emperor's spies could be anywhere.

Victor and Scott were in the same social studies class, and Victor couldn't wait to give him the good news about Ben.

If Victor could find his classroom.

By the time he located it, down a side hall behind the cafeteria, class had already begun. The teacher, a short redheaded woman named Mrs. Kerwin, was finishing attendance when Victor stumbled in.

"And you are?" she said, peering over the rims of her reading glasses.

"Uh, I'm Victor Godwin. Sorry I'm late."

"'You may delay, but time will not.' Class begins precisely at eight. Please try to remember that."

"I will." Victor wound his way to the empty desk behind Angela Willbrant. Scott was seated one row over, a few seats behind. Victor pointed to imaginary bolts on his neck and gave Scott a thumbs-up sign to let him know Franklin was okay.

"This year, we will begin by studying early American history and the founders of our country. I consider it one of the most fascinating periods in history. It also happens to be a specialty of mine." Mrs. Kerwin bowed modestly. "Over the course of this year, I will attempt to bring the founding fathers to life for you."

Victor chuckled. If she only knew!

"Mr. Godwin, did I say something funny?"

"No, Mrs. Kerwin. I'm so sorry. I was just thinking of a friend of mine."

"I see. This friend of yours, does he have a habit of showing up late and causing a distraction?"

"Uh . . . well, he kind of does," admitted Victor.

"Victor, when you first walked in, I told you that you may delay, but time will not. Do you know what that means?"

"I think so."

"And do you know who said it?"

"I'm not sure."

"A man named Benjamin Franklin, one of the greatest minds our country has produced. You would do well to get to know him a little better."

This time it was Scott's turn to laugh.

Mrs. Kerwin scowled and cleared her throat. "Now then, can anyone tell me something about Dr. Franklin?"

"He's on the fifty dollar bill," offered Hanna O'Brien.

"Actually, Franklin is on the hundred," said Mrs. Kerwin. "Anything else?"

"He was a president," said Cody Quinn.

"He was *not* a president," said Mrs. Kerwin. "Although he was a statesman, a diplomat, a writer, a scientist, and an inventor. Can anyone name one of his inventions?"

"The bioptiscope!" said Scott. Victor shot him a nasty look.

"Franklin did *not* invent the bioptiscope, whatever that is." Mrs. Kerwin massaged her temples and let out a long sigh. "I can see we have a lot of work to do this year."

Victor raised his hand. "I can tell you something Franklin invented."

"Yes?"

"Swimming flippers. But he wore them on his hands."

The class laughed, but Mrs. Kerwin's eyes grew wide. "That's absolutely correct, Victor. Where did you learn that?"

"From my friend, the one I told you about before. He's kind of an expert on Benjamin Franklin."

"Marvelous," said Mrs. Kerwin. "Perhaps there's hope for you yet."

The rest of class went by quickly. Just before the end, Mrs. Kerwin ducked into the closet and emerged with a large cardboard box.

"In the spirit of invention, I have a special surprise gift for everyone."

The class leaned forward in anticipation.

"Lightbulbs!" announced Mrs. Kerwin.

The class slumped back in their chairs with a collective groan.

"But not just *any* bulbs," she continued. "Infinity Bulbs! The Infinity Unlimited Company has generously donated four of these amazing devices to every child in our public schools. They use practically no electricity, are great for the environment, and will save your families money on their electrical bills. You may each take a box as you leave."

"Do we have to?" asked Denny Berkus.

"'A penny saved is a penny earned,'" said Mrs. Kerwin. "So yes, you have to."

That afternoon, riding home on the bus, Victor received a puzzling text message.

```
m u r 0 c n — n r l o
e h n t c a s e o e t
e q e h l t u l m r h
t o r a e 7 n a a t e
a n o n l : s u t t r
t c f d l 3 h n . h s
p o 2 m a 0 i d a e .
```

"What in the world is that?" asked Scott.

Victor studied his phone for a moment. "It's a message from Jaime. We're going to need your dad's help. Can you guys pick me up around seven tonight?"

CHAPTER FOUR
Science Club

That evening after dinner, Victor and his mother sat on their couch to watch the six o'clock news. "So how was the first day of school, kiddo?" Mrs. Godwin asked.

"Okay, I guess. My new social studies teacher, Mrs. Kerwin? She's going to be tough."

Mrs. Godwin smiled. "Well, honey, sometimes the tough teachers are the ones we learn the most from."

Victor reached into his backpack and pulled out a box. "She handed out these Infinity Bulbs to everybody in the class. They're supposed to save energy."

"I love these," Mrs. Godwin said, taking the box. "In fact, I've already replaced most of our old bulbs with them. Hey, look—they're talking about them on TV."

WURP news reporter Katy Kaitlyn appeared on the television screen.

"In local news, it looks like inventor and owner of Infinity Unlimited, Ed Thomason, is about to add 'good citizen' to his list of accomplishments. Earlier today, he held a press conference to announce the next phase in what sounds to us like a pretty bright idea!"

The image switched to that of a very old man standing at a podium on the front steps of Independence Hall. The wind tousled his unruly white hair. Victor thought he looked oddly familiar. The man began to speak.

"Ladies and gentlemen, in this very building behind me, our great country was founded on the principle of freedom. I stand here to offer a new kind of freedom: freedom from expensive energy bills.

"Recently, I've begun supplying thousands of Infinity Bulbs to the City of Philadelphia. You've probably already noticed them in your parks, schools, streets, and government buildings. And for weeks, Infinity Bulbs have been available in stores at affordable prices. But from this point on, Infinity Bulbs are yours for free. Simply visit any store and turn in your old lightbulbs. Then take as many Infinity Bulbs as you need. This is my gift to you, citizens of Philadelphia, the city of freedom!"

"Those *are* great bulbs," Mrs. Godwin said. "Everyone should get them."

The television image switched back to Katy Kaitlyn: *"Exactly how the Infinity Bulbs produce so much light from so little power remains a mystery. Mr. Thomason calls it a company secret. And now, to the weather with Skip!"*

Victor winced as his best friend's father jumped onto the screen. He was wearing a mask and a gaudy professional wrestling costume. The words WEATHER WRESTLER were printed on the back of his cape. An actor wearing a fluffy gray cloud costume snuck up behind him and jumped on his back. Skip flipped the cloud over his shoulder and pinned him to the studio floor.

"Take that, rain cloud!"

The rain cloud groaned.

"I really like Mr. Weaver," Victor said, "but as a scientist, I can only take his weather forecasts in small doses."

Victor's mom turned off the television. "You'd better get your homework done. The others will be here soon to take you to your science club." She turned on the lamp next to her and picked up a book.

. . . relax . . .

"Mom, did you just hear something?"

"Like what?"

SKIP WEAVER'S FAVORITE COSTUME PROPS

- *Battery-Operated Bow Tie*
- *Waterproof Tuxedo*
- *Exploding Shoes with Sparkler Socks*

- *Double-Breasted Overalls*
- *Parachute Pants with Grappling Hook*
- *Inflatable Thundershorts*

"Like a voice?" Victor asked.

"No. Why, did you hear something?"

Victor shrugged. "I thought I did."

A little after seven o'clock, the doorbell rang. Victor found his mom in the living room, still sitting on the couch. "That's Scott. I shouldn't be long."

Mrs. Godwin didn't answer. Her book was open on her lap, but it didn't look like she was reading it.

"Mom?" Victor touched her shoulder. "Scott's here."

"Huh?" Mrs. Godwin started. "Oh, sorry, honey. My mind must have been elsewhere. Have fun at your science club. I'm picking up a few extra hours at work tonight. Make sure you're home by nine. If there's an emergency, call Mrs. Vamos next door."

Victor felt bad about not being 100 percent honest with his mom about where he was going. But the Promethean Underground had to remain a secret. And technically it *was* a kind of science club.

Downstairs, Scott was waiting at the door. Victor followed him to the WURP news van. "Howdy, Victor!" said Skip Weaver. He was still dressed as the Weather Wrestler.

"Hi, Mr. Weaver." Victor climbed into the back and sat next to Scott.

"Did you catch my dad's forecast?" Scott asked.

"Only the beginning," Victor said. "Who won?"

"My dad, of course!" Scott said. "And guess what? He sent the cloud to the hospital—for real!"

"It was only a minor sprain," Skip said, sounding a little embarrassed. "So where exactly are we going?"

"According to the text I got, we're being called to a meeting at Promethean Underground Headquarters on the corner of 20th and McClellan."

"That's near the place where I buy my capes," Skip said. "Let's go!"

Mr. Weaver hit the gas and pulled out into traffic. He drove the same way he gave his weather forecasts—as if he didn't care who was watching. The streets of Philadelphia flew by in a dizzying blur. For the second time in the same week, Victor wished he had brought a barf bag.

"I wonder what Promethean Underground Headquarters looks like," said Scott. "Maybe it's—"

. . . obey . . .

Skip, Scott, and Victor all flinched at the same time.

"Hey!" Victor said, noticing the others' reactions. "Did you guys hear that too?"

"You mean 'obey'?" Scott asked. "Yeah, I thought it was just me. I've been hearing whispers all day."

"Same here," Skip said. "Weird. Hey, here we are!"

Skip parked the van on the sidewalk. "Are you sure you

got the address right? This building looks kind of run-down for a secret headquarters."

"Read the text I got." Victor pushed a few buttons on his phone and brought up the message:

```
m u r 0 c n — n r l o
e h n t c a s e o e t
e q e h l t u l m r h
t o r a e 7 n a a t e
a n o n l : s u t t r
t c f d l 3 h n . h s
p o 2 m a 0 i d a e .
```

Skip scratched his head. "I don't get it."

"Wait, it's a code, right?" Scott said excitedly.

"Exactly," Victor said. "The trick is not to read it from left to right, but from top to bottom, one column at a time. Try it."

Slowly Skip sounded out the message: *"'Meet at PU . . .'"*

Scott snickered and held his nose. *"Pee-yew!"*

"I know!" Skip laughed. "But there's more." He continued reading. *"Meet at PUHQ on corner of 20th and McClellan at 7:30—Sunshine Laundromat. Alert the others.'"*

They peered across the street at the Sunshine Laundromat. Garbage littered the sidewalk. Its large plate-glass window was streaked with grease and mud. Almost every other letter on its neon sign had blown out, and the front door hung crooked on its hinge. A sign read CLOSED.

They crossed the street and knocked.

CHAPTER FIVE
The Promethean Underground

They waited a minute and then knocked again. They heard the sound of dead bolts unlocking and chains sliding from the other side. The door opened a crack and a hunched-over old woman peeked out. She frowned. "We're closed," she barked, pointing at the sign. "Can't you read?"

"I'm Victor Godwin, and these are my friends Scott and his dad, Skip," Victor explained. "We were told to come here for a meeting."

"There's no meeting here," the old woman said.

She slammed the door.

"That didn't go so well," Skip said. "Maybe this is just a Laundromat, like the sign says."

Victor thought for a moment. "I have an idea."

He knocked on the door again. It opened.

"Get out of here, you hoodlums, or I'll call the cops!" the old woman snapped.

Victor held up his phone and showed her the message.

The old woman looked up and down the street. "Quickly, come in."

Skip and Scott looked at each other, then followed Victor inside.

The old woman shut the door behind her and locked it. "Forgive me," she said, leading them briskly down a hallway, "but we must take precautions. The Emperor has spies and saboteurs everywhere."

They passed through a dark, dingy room filled with a half-dozen washers and dryers. At the back, the old woman opened the glass door to an industrial-size washing machine. "Climb inside, please, Mr. Weaver."

Skip looked at the washer. "Seriously?"

"Please," the old woman answered.

Skip shrugged and climbed inside. The woman pressed the Start button three times quickly and then held it for several seconds. There was a loud *thunk,* and the machine shuddered. When she opened the door, Skip was gone.

"Cool!" Scott said. "I'm next!"

Scott climbed in. The woman closed the door and pushed the button again. She opened the door and Scott had vanished too.

"That leaves you, Victor," the old woman said.

Cautiously, he climbed inside the washing machine. The door clicked behind him. The machine began to shake, and a panel opened up. He fell backward and tumbled down a slide onto a basement floor. Skip and Scott were there, dusting off their pants, and next to them stood . . .

"Ben!" Victor exclaimed. "They fixed you!"

Franklin beamed at Victor. "New *and* improved—I even have a new battery belt, thanks to our fellow Promethean

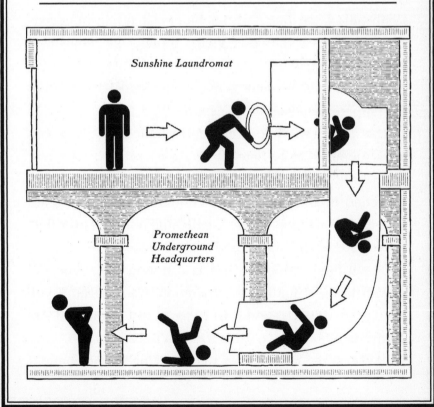

PUHQ *Secret Washing Machine Entrance*

Sunshine Laundromat

*Promethean
Underground
Headquarters*

scientists! Now follow me, gentlemen. There are some people I'd like you to meet."

Franklin led them into the next room. It was much bigger than the Laundromat upstairs. Machines and glass cabinets filled with chemicals lined the walls. In one corner a group of people were gathered around a large table covered with blueprints, maps, and computers.

"Wander around and have a look," Franklin said, "but don't touch anything. Ms. Aldini will be here in a moment."

While Skip and Franklin chatted, Victor and Scott explored the room. Two Promethean scientists had disassembled a large piece of machinery. It lay in hundreds of pieces across the floor. Victor thought he recognized some of the parts.

"Pardon me," he said to one of the scientists. "Is that the Emperor's harmonic transmitter?"

The man eyed Victor and Scott suspiciously. "Are you boys supposed to be here?"

The old woman from the Sunshine Laundromat approached them. "It's okay, Dr. Anthony. These boys are here for the meeting. I have the distinct honor of introducing you to Victor Godwin and Scott Weaver."

Dr. Anthony smiled. "It's a real honor, boys. You did a great thing in finding the harmonic transmitter. If you hadn't . . . well, I shudder to think of it. I'm Dr. Walt Anthony, and this is my partner, Dr. Ella DeLacey."

"A pleasure," Dr. DeLacey said, shaking Victor's hand.

PARTS OF THE HARMONIC TRANSMITTER

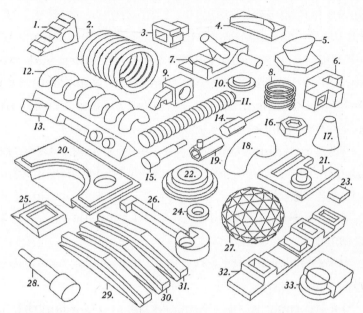

1. Wedge bracket	12. Accelerating bumpuses (7)	23. Numerating clock box
2. Harmonic coil	13. Limiting wedge	24. Photon ring
3. Oscillating widget	14. Linchpin	25. Rhombus wedge
4. Wheel casing	15. Ionizing propellant cap	26. Overhead cam assembly
5. Amplifying collar	16. Fishnut (metric)	27. Mesmerizing egg
6. Stabilizing bracket	17. Electrifying fez	28. Electrophonic tuner
7. Throttleblock	18. Marconi noodle	29. Tuning brace
8. Harmonic sub-coil	19. Oscillating fob	30. Harmonic brace
9. Electromagnetometer	20. Depressed flange	31. Enharmonic brace
10. Radiating cap insulator	21. Edison jackbracket	32. Unifying slot assembly
11. Elephant spring	22. Recharging plate	33. Shocking slipswitcher

Scott looked at the pieces scattered across the floor. "You guys really broke it good. I bet the Emperor's mad."

Dr. DeLacey laughed. "I'd like to think so. But we've received word that he's building a new transmitter. Only this one will be much more powerful."

Franklin and Skip joined them, along with a scientist Victor recognized from the Promethean testing area. "Victor, Scott," Dr. Gwynn said. He nodded toward the old woman from the Laundromat. "I see you've met Ms. Nina Aldini. She's the leader of the Promethean Underground."

"Wow!" Skip said.

"It's not as impressive as it sounds," Ms. Aldini replied. She gestured around the room. "I'm afraid this little group is all we have."

"And the Wright brothers," Dr. DeLacey added. "They're on patrol."

"Now I'm afraid we have little time," Ms. Aldini said. "Please follow me."

She led them to the corner of the room, where Victor spotted a familiar face.

"Hi, Jaime," he called.

Jaime Winters sat behind a computer, studying the screen. She looked up. "Hi, guys. Glad you made it."

"Let's begin," Ms. Aldini said. "We all know why the Modern Order of Prometheus was created. If civilization ever faced a Great Emergency, we could awaken history's most revered inventors to save the day. Today, a Great Emergency is upon us. Unfortunately, the Order *is* that emergency.

"Somehow, over the years, the Emperor has slowly taken control of the Modern Order of Prometheus. Our scientists have been disappearing, and we've lost contact with almost all of our Custodians and the inventors they cared for.

"We don't know who the Emperor is, but we do know that he's devious. Thanks to our guests, his plan to force the Wright brothers to hypnotize Philadelphia failed. But since then, we've learned that he has devised another, more cunning plan. Jaime, bring up the video."

The WURP website appeared projected on the wall. Jaime clicked on a link that read **Infinity Bulbs Free for Philadelphia**. A video of the news conference began to run. It was the same one Victor and his mom had watched earlier.

"Pause it right there, Jaime," Ms. Aldini said. "Does anyone recognize that man?"

"Absolutely," Skip said. "That's Ed Thomason. He's a genius. He invented the Infinity Bulb."

Ms. Aldini shook her head. "That man is *not* Ed Thomason. Victor, I understand you know quite a bit about the inventors of the past. Do you recognize him?"

"Of course!" Victor said, slapping his forehead. "Thomas Alva Edison—the inventor of the lightbulb. Why didn't I recognize him before?"

"Correct. Edison was preserved by the Modern Order of Prometheus in 1931. Now he is awake. But *we* did not wake him up."

1243.57 6131.00
0015.44 0011.21
313... 718.52

CHAPTER SIX

The Emperor's Plan

"*We believe that* the Emperor is able to awaken inventors from his headquarters using something called broadcast power," Dr. Gwynn said.

"I've heard of that," Victor said.

Jaime clicked a button and a diagram of an antenna appeared on the wall.

"It's an amazing technology," Dr. Anthony explained. "An inventor named Nikola Tesla proposed it a long time ago. He believed that electricity could be transmitted through the air like radio waves. He even demonstrated it in public, but it was limited to low power and short distances. We believe those limits no longer exist."

"Victor," Franklin said, "you told me that the night I

awoke from my Leyden casket, there was a flash of lightning that struck only your house. These scientists believe it was actually a blast of broadcast power from the Emperor."

"I *knew* there was something strange about that lightning strike!" Victor said. "So that's how he woke up the Wright brothers."

"And now Thomas Edison," Ms. Aldini confirmed. "We believe the Emperor is controlling him, just as he once did Orville and Wilbur."

Victor had a curious look on his face. "But I still don't understand, Ben. How come he wasn't able to control you?"

"Because of you, Victor," Franklin said. "When each inventor awoke, power from our Leyden caskets still flowed through our veins for a short time. Our Custodians were supposed to recharge us and adjust the harmonic systems immediately. Without their Custodian, the Wright brothers' power drained away, making them unexpectedly vulnerable to the Emperor's control. Now Edison shares that same fate."

"But your Custodian was missing too," Scott said. "Mr. Mercer died before you woke up."

"Murdered," Franklin said grimly. "With him gone, I also should have become the Emperor's puppet. But my power never fully ran out."

"The battery belt!" Scott said.

"Exactly."

"Victor, you saved Ben!"

Victor beamed.

"So what happened to Edison's Custodian?" asked Skip.

"Custodians," Jaime said softly.

"Jaime's parents were both in charge of Edison," Dr. Anthony explained. "They vanished at the same time he did."

"I'm so sorry," said Skip.

No one spoke for a moment.

Jaime broke the silence. "My mom and dad took their job very seriously. Just like my grandparents, and my great-grandparents before them. In a weird way, Edison has always felt like a member of our family."

"And we have a plan to get them all back," Ms. Aldini said. Jaime clicked a button and a picture of an Infinity Bulb appeared on the wall. "Ella, can you fill everyone in on where we stand?"

Dr. DeLacey stood up. "We believe that the Emperor awakened Edison in order to make him invent the Infinity Bulb. Together, they have done an astounding job of installing these bulbs throughout Philadelphia. They are in homes, stores, traffic lights—everywhere."

"They even installed all new lights at the TV station," Skip added. "No charge!"

"What's so special about the bulbs?" Victor asked.

"Our theory," Dr. DeLacey said, "is that the Emperor is using Infinity Bulbs to spy on people. We think they're listening devices."

"But you don't listen with lightbulbs," Scott said. "You listen with microphones."

"We believe Infinity Bulbs are a kind of microphone," Dr. Gwynn explained.

"But it's easier to convince people to put free lightbulbs in their houses than free microphones," Jaime said.

"Besides, these aren't ordinary microphones," Ms. Aldini continued. "We suspect they are monitoring more than just sound."

"Like what?"

"We're not sure. The Emperor may be able to see through them, monitor people's locations, tap into their computer networks . . . The possibilities are endless."

"What does he want?" Scott asked.

"Knowledge is power," Jaime answered. "He can use all of that secret information to control the city."

"Nefarious!" Franklin declared. "A diabolical corruption of science."

"We've been struggling to understand exactly how Infinity Bulbs work," Ms. Aldini said. "You're here because we need your help—all of you."

"What can we do?" Skip asked.

"Mr. Weaver, you have access to WURP's news feed. We need you to monitor the situation from the station. If you hear reports of anything strange happening, contact us immediately." Ms. Aldini handed him a cell phone. "Use this. Just press 4-3-2-1 and I'll answer."

"Right," Skip said. He pulled a notepad out of his pocket and mumbled as he wrote: "Four, three, two, one . . ."

"Victor, we need for you and Dr. Franklin to study what makes Infinity Bulbs work. You might be able to learn something that we missed."

"What about me?" Scott asked.

Ms. Aldini thought for a moment. "Hmm, yes. Scott, your task is very important. It's, uh . . . We need you to, uh . . ."

"You're emergency backup, Scott," Jaime said. "In case any one of us needs help."

"Like a volunteer fireman?" Scott said.

"Exactly!" Ms. Aldini said. "In the meantime, a couple of us plan to sneak into the Infinity Unlimited factory tonight. Jaime, bring up the computer model and show them what we've got so far."

A three-dimensional image of the Infinity Unlimited factory appeared on the wall.

"It's based on photographs that Orville and Wilbur took from their gyroplanes." Jaime clicked and twirled the building around. "There are four visible main levels, and probably a basement."

"We'll know more tonight, once we're inside," Dr. Anthony said. "We'll collect as much information as we can. Hopefully, that will help us stop the Emperor."

"That sounds dangerous," Scott said.

"Extremely dangerous," Ms. Aldini confirmed. "Let's meet again tomorrow at four to share what we've all

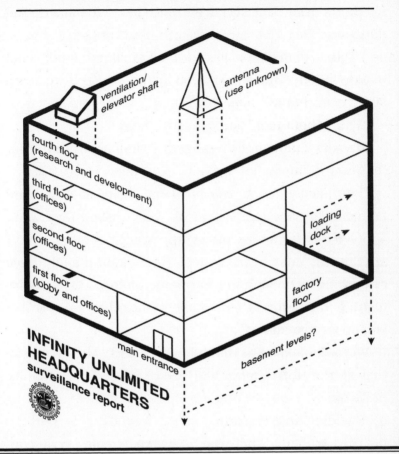

ventilation/
elevator shaft

antenna
(use unknown)

fourth floor
(research and development)

third floor
(offices)

second floor
(offices)

loading
dock

first floor
(lobby and offices)

factory
floor

INFINITY UNLIMITED
HEADQUARTERS
surveillance report

main entrance

basement levels?

learned." She looked at the clock. "Now you boys had better get home. It's late."

During the drive home, Victor leaned his tired head against
the window as the night's revelations whirled around

inside his brain. The secret entrance into Promethean Underground Headquarters . . . lightbulbs that spy on you . . . and Thomas Edison? It was a lot to take in.

Skip stopped the van at a red light.

. . . concentrate . . . for instructions . . . prepare . . .

"There it is again," said Scott. "Creepy."

Franklin snapped his head up. "You all heard that?"

"You too?"

"I've been hearing voices in my head all day," said Franklin. "Orville and Wilbur as well. I asked Dr. Gwynn about it. As far as he knows, the Wright brothers and I are the only ones hearing them. He thought it might have something to do with our harmonic biology. But if you're hearing them too, there must be another reason. We should let him know."

Victor looked up at the red light. "Didn't Ms. Aldini say that all the traffic lights had been replaced with Infinity Bulbs?"

"She did," said Franklin.

"I just had an idea. These bulbs are listening in on conversations, right? Then they're broadcasting what they hear back to the Emperor. What if, somehow, we're picking up parts of those broadcasts?"

"But we're not harmonical, like Ben and the Wright brothers," said Scott. "Why can we hear them too?"

"That's a very good question," said Victor.

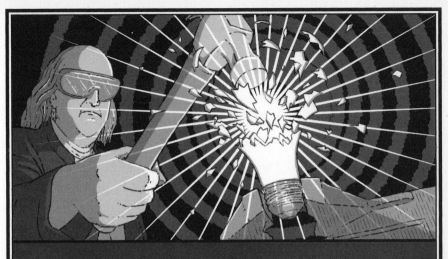

CHAPTER SEVEN
Shouting at Lightbulbs

Back at home, Victor and Franklin paused outside Franklin's apartment door to compare notes.

"Since it is a school night," said Franklin, "I propose that I begin analyzing the bulbs now, and you join me as soon as you get home tomorrow."

"Actually, my mom's working late tonight," said Victor. "How about we do a little work right now?"

Franklin pulled a ring of keys from his pocket and began to sort through them. "Out of the question. You need to get your rest. The Prometheans can do without you for one night."

"My mom made cupcakes," said Victor.

Franklin paused, the key turned halfway in the door lock.

"And we could just work for a little while," added Victor. "Say, a half hour?"

Franklin nodded. "A half an hour, no more. After all, early to bed, early to rise, makes a man—"

"I know: 'healthy, wealthy, and wise,'" said Victor, bounding up the stairs. "I'll be right down."

Twenty minutes later, Victor returned carrying a large cardboard box, his laptop bag slung over his shoulder.

"Sorry to take so long," he said. "I just thought it would be a good idea to remove all the Infinity Bulbs from our apartment. I've got them in the box here, in case we need some extras to study."

"A wise precaution," said Franklin. He peered into the box, a growing look of concern on his face. "But what about . . . ?"

"The cupcakes are in a container underneath," said Victor.

"Very good!" said Franklin. "Let us begin."

Victor followed the old man into the living room, behind the secret bookcase, and down into the basement. A lot had changed in the months since he had first discovered the dusty old laboratory. Together, he and Franklin had upgraded much of the equipment, installed wireless Internet, and even added a basic security system.

Franklin cleared off a space on a large worktable and began to collect the testing equipment.

"Here's the big problem, as I see it," said Victor. "If these bulbs are listening devices, then how can we test them without the Emperor knowing what we're doing? Once we plug them in, he'll be able to hear us."

"An interesting question," said Franklin. He took a bite of a cupcake. "How exactly do you suppose they deliver their information back to the Emperor?"

"I know it's possible to set up a local computer network through the outlets in your house. I suppose it would also be possible to create a big network from the electrical grid across the entire city."

"So if we use power that is not connected to the city's electrical grid, the Emperor should not be able to hear us," said Franklin. He pointed toward a harmonic Leyden jar, a special battery invented by the Prometheans.

"Great idea." Victor unspooled a coil of wire and began to rig up a basic circuit. When he connected the last wire, the Infinity Bulb began to glow softly.

"Excellent!" said Franklin. "Now, if this bulb is indeed a type of microphone, we should see some change in the electricity running through the circuit when I speak into it. A sort of hidden signal, correct?"

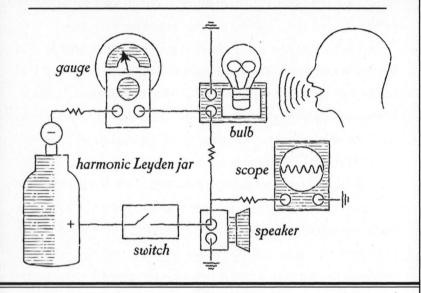

"Exactly," said Victor. "And I have some ideas about how we can find that signal."

The two scientists set to work, connecting a variety of speakers, scopes, and gauges to the circuit in an effort to identify anything out of the ordinary. But no matter how loudly they shouted at the lightbulb, the signal remained flat. An hour later, they were out of both ideas and cupcakes.

"Perhaps we are going about this the wrong way," said Franklin. "Instead of studying how the bulb works, maybe we should be studying the bulb itself. Let's take one apart."

Victor took one of the Infinity Bulbs from the box and delicately secured it in a vise. He studied it for a moment.

"Just one question. How exactly do you take a lightbulb apart?"

"Like this!" said Franklin. He picked up a small tack hammer from the workbench and tapped the top of the bulb. The glass made a metallic sound, but didn't crack. Franklin tapped it harder.

"Interesting."

"Very," said Victor.

"Stand back." Franklin struck the bulb hard, and the glass finally shattered. The impact was followed immediately by a puff of black smoke and a high-pitched hissing sound.

Victor stepped forward and examined what remained of the bulb. The metal base was still fixed in the vise, but everything inside the bulb had disintegrated into a fine black powder.

Victor gasped. "I don't believe it. It completely self-destructed!"

CUPCAKE

frosting

jelly bean

sprinkles

paper baking cup

cake

CHAPTER EIGHT
Skipping School

Victor's head throbbed with every lurching stop and start of the school bus.

It had been a long night. He and Franklin had gone through the entire box of Infinity Bulbs, yet were no closer to understanding how they worked. Now, exhausted, he faced a twenty-five-minute ride to school on the oldest, most beat-up bus on the planet.

"It's not fair," said Scott.

"What's not fair?"

"Jaime's our age. She should have to go to school too."

The rear tire struck a pothole and tossed the boys up, then painfully back down onto their seat. Victor felt his breakfast turn over in his stomach.

"Jaime's homeschooled by her parents. Or at least, she was."

Scott nodded. "Oh yeah."

Victor closed his eyes and took a long deep breath, then gagged. The pungent smell of gasoline filled his nose.

"I wish I were homeschooled," said Scott. "My dad knows tons of stuff."

"He certainly would make an interesting teacher," Victor agreed. Just that morning, Skip Weaver had delivered his weather forecast in a bikini. Evidently it had something to do with saying good-bye to summer.

The school bus jerked to a stop and two high school girls got on. They stumbled to the back and collapsed onto a seat.

"Hey, they look more tired than you," said Scott.

Victor glanced around at the other passengers. "Everyone does. Even the driver." The bus started up again and immediately bounced onto the curb.

"You know what's funny?"

"What?" said Victor.

Scott pointed to the ceiling. "It's sunny outside, but the driver's so sleepy, he left all the lights on inside the bus."

The second they walked into school, Victor knew that something was wrong.

"What's going on?" whispered Scott.

"No idea," said Victor. "This is weird."

All around, teachers and students were going about their morning routines, opening their lockers, getting ready for the day. But somehow, everything was *less* than usual. People were walking slower, their movements more deliberate, their eyes glazed over.

And no one was talking.

"It's like they need new batteries," Scott whispered.

"Exactly," said Victor.

. . . *relax* . . .

"There it is again," whispered Scott.

Victor nodded. "But it doesn't look like anyone else heard it." Up and down the hall, business at Philo T. Farnsworth Middle School continued uninterrupted.

"I wonder why not," said Scott.

"That's a good question," said Victor. He sidestepped a girl who was standing in place, lost in a daze. "It's almost like we're radios, and we're tuned to a station that no one else can hear. Or . . ."

He paused and looked up at the ceiling, where a row of Infinity Bulbs glowed brightly.

"Or what?" said Scott.

"Or maybe everyone else *can* hear the station. They just don't know they can!" Victor's eyes grew wide. "Scott, what if we've been going about this all wrong? What if the Infinity Bulbs aren't for listening—what if they're for *sending* messages?"

Scott wrinkled his nose. "I don't get it."

"Okay, this might sound a little crazy, but hear me out. Remember last month at the art park? When your dad rolled the van with the charging sphere into the Megabat?"

"That was awesome!" said Scott. "And remember when—"

"I'm not done," said Victor. "There was a bright flash, and then a loud noise. Now think carefully—do you remember anything immediately after that?"

"I remember I felt really weird for a second."

"Exactly," said Victor. "Me too. Like we were exposed to something."

"Exposed? Like to the flu?"

"More like to a wave of energy. The same harmonic energy that Ben and the other inventors have flowing through their veins."

"I don't get it," said Scott.

"Look," whispered Victor, "we know that the harmonic fluid in Ben's body makes him function like an antenna. What if the same thing is happening to us, just at a lower level?"

"Wait, I'm confused. You're saying we're radio antennas?"

"I'm saying that maybe *everyone* is. But because of the harmonic blast, *our* radios are more sensitive than everyone else's. Sensitive enough to hear things other people just sense subliminally."

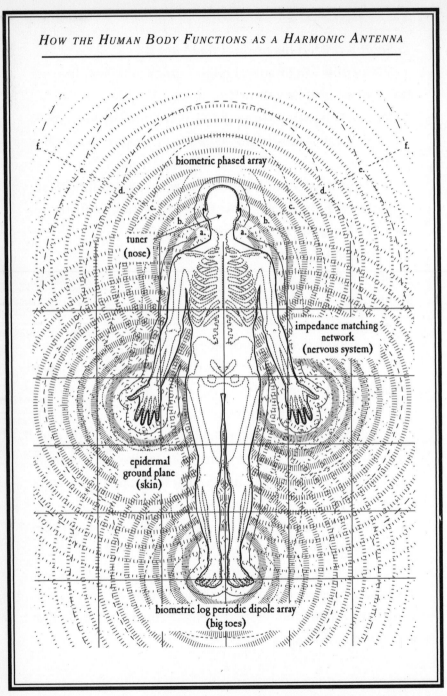

biometric phased array

tuner
(nose)

impedance matching
network
(nervous system)

epidermal
ground plane
(skin)

biometric log periodic dipole array
(big toes)

"Sub*what*?"

"*Subliminally.* It means they hear the messages without knowing they're hearing them. They're being *hypnotized.*"

Scott nodded. "I think I get it. So you, me, and my dad can hear the voices because we were at the explosion . . ."

". . . and Ben and the Wright brothers hear it because they're full of harmonic fluid," said Victor. "But we're not hearing voices. We're just hearing *one* voice."

"Edison? You think he's the one saying all that stuff?"

"No—the Emperor. He's the one pulling all the strings. We need to let Jaime know right away." Victor pulled out his phone and studied the screen.

"What's wrong?"

"Jaime sent a text. There's some sort of problem. She wants us to meet her at the bus stop near the Infinity Bulb factory."

"When?"

"Right now. But obviously we can't skip school."

Scott gave him an annoyed look. "To save Philadelphia? Are you kidding?"

"I don't know . . . ," said Victor.

"It's easy. Just follow my lead."

Scott opened the door to the classroom, and they stepped inside. Mrs. Kerwin stood at the front of the room. Across the chalkboard, she had written the words *Silent study time. Relax.* The students who had already arrived were sitting sleepily at their desks, gazing at their textbooks. Some of the textbooks were still closed.

"Maybe I should call my mom," whispered Victor. "She could call the office and—"

"Hold on—let me try something." Scott walked to the front of the room. "Mrs. Kerwin, Victor and I need to leave for a little while."

Mrs. Kerwin smiled and nodded.

Scott winked at Victor, and the two of them turned and walked out of the room, then straight out of the school.

MEANWHILE . . .

The bell above the door rang as a tall man walked into Ernie's Hardware Store.

Ernie peered over the top of his well-thumbed copy of *Unpopular Science*. "Howdy, future satisfied customer! What can I do ya for?"

The man surveyed the store. From wall to wall, its shelves were packed with just about everything he needed to complete his invention.

"I've been to several supply houses looking for very specific equipment but have not been able to find it," the man said. "I've been told that whatever they don't have, you stock."

Ernie stared at the man for a moment. "Hey, I know you!

You're that guy from the TV. The forever lightbulb guy, what was it? Al Tomkinson, right?"

The man smiled. "Ed Thomason. And you're thinking of my invention, the Infinity Bulb. Pleased to make your acquaintance."

"Sure, sure!" Ernie said, grinning. "It's a real pleasure. So what do you need?"

The man took a long list out of his pocket and read off two dozen items.

"Yeah, I've got all of that," Ernie said. "Give me a few minutes and I'll pull it together."

Ernie scurried around the store, grabbing up armfuls of titanium-reinforced tubes, hexagonal cogs, beryllium switches, four fireplace bellows, magnetic springs, woofer speakers, an old Victrola, and the list went on. When he finally gathered everything, he dumped it all in a pile on the floor in front of the counter and wiped his forehead with a polka-dotted handkerchief.

"There you go, Mr. Thomason. Let me ring you up." Ernie went behind the counter and tapped away at a calculator. "That'll be eleven hundred dollars. Wow, more expensive than I thought. But you pay for the best, am I right? Cash or charge?"

The man pointed behind the counter. "Is that an automobile battery?"

"Sure is," Ernie said. "Do you want to see it?"

"Please."

Ernie lifted it up and set it on the counter in front of the man.

"Is it fully charged?" he asked.

"Absotively!"

"Excellent." He stuck both fingers in his mouth, licked them, and then touched the positive and negative terminals on the battery.

"Hey, wait!" To Ernie's astonishment, the smiling man began to glow. Softly at first, then bright white, and then soft again. The pulse was relaxing, soothing, hypnotic . . .

"I am a nice man," Ed Thomason intoned. *"You like me."*

"I . . . like you," Ernie said, gazing into the glow.

"You don't want to charge me for this equipment."

"I don't want to charge you for this equipment."

"You want to take it outside and load it into the white truck."

"I want to take it outside and load it into the white truck."

"It was a pleasure doing business with me."

"It was a pleasure doing business with you!"

CHAPTER NINE
Plan B: Costumes!

Victor and Scott stepped off the bus a block from the Infinity Unlimited factory. Jaime was waiting for them on a bench. She wore sunglasses and was dressed entirely in black, as usual. At her feet were two enormous suitcases and a backpack.

"Hi, Jaime," said Victor. He glanced up and down the sidewalk. "What's going on? You said there was a problem."

Jaime motioned the two of them closer. Victor could see she was shaking. "Dr. Anthony and Dr. DeLacey never returned from the mission. I came here to check on them, and when I got back to headquarters, Dr. Gwynn and Ms. Aldini were gone too."

"Did anyone leave a message?"

"No. And they're not answering their phones."

Victor frowned. "I think I may know what happened to them." He went on to explain his theory about the voices they'd been hearing and how the Emperor was using the Infinity Bulbs to hypnotize people.

Jaime watched the pedestrians walking up and down the sidewalk. They moved slowly, with blank, emotionless faces. "They do look kind of out of it," she said.

"Exactly," said Victor. "They're in a hypnotic trance, just like the people at our school."

"But I haven't been hearing any mysterious voices," said Jaime. "Why haven't I been hypnotized?"

"I don't know," said Victor.

Jaime sighed. "I was afraid the team had been captured, but hypnotized? That's far worse." She looked down the street. A block away, the Infinity Unlimited logo was mounted on a long brick building. "I'm going in to check things out."

"By yourself?"

"We'll help, won't we, Victor?" said Scott.

"I, uh . . . Of course we will."

"Thanks, guys," said Jaime. "We knew we could count on you."

"We?" said Scott.

"Dr. Franklin should be here any minute."

"You let him travel through the city on his own?" asked Victor. "Do you think that's wise?"

Jaime shrugged. "I can't tell him what to do."

"Yes, but—"

Victor felt a tap on his shoulder. "Excuse me, young man. Can you tell me how to get to the busport?"

Victor spun around and was face-to-face with a peculiar figure. The man wore a baseball cap, sunglasses, Hawaiian shirt, plaid shorts, dark socks, and sandals. A large camera hung around his neck, and he was intently studying a map of the city.

"Ben?"

"I'm sorry," said the man. "My name is, er, Charlie. I'm from out of the town and I'm a little lost."

Victor sighed. "Ben, I know it's you."

The old man's face fell. "How could you tell?"

"First of all, there's no such thing as a busport. There's a bus *stop* or an *air*port. The phrase is 'out of town,' not 'out of *the* town.' And finally, no one, not even a tourist, actually dresses like that. What in the world are you doing?"

"It is our plan for sneaking into the factory," said Franklin. "We devised it this morning."

Victor glanced at Jaime, who shook her head. "By any chance, did Mr. Weaver have something to do with this?"

"Absolutely! It was his idea," said Franklin. "How could you tell?"

"My dad knows all about costumes," explained Scott. "Once he dressed up as a gorilla for my cousin's birthday and she didn't recognize him, even when the police came."

Victor sat down on the bench and turned to Jaime. "And how exactly is this supposed to get us into the factory?"

"It's the best we could come up with on short notice," Jaime said with a sigh. "Here, put these on." She handed Victor two small bundles of cloth.

"What are they?"

"Black pants and T-shirt, for disappearing into the shadows once we get inside. You can change behind the tree over there."

Victor examined the clothes skeptically. "These look too small. Where did you get them?"

"Just put them on," said Jaime.

"Hey, look!" said Scott. He held up a pair of Liberty Bell–shaped sunglasses. "I get a costume too."

"We're all in costume—it's part of the plan!" said Franklin proudly. "Now do hurry, Victor. We haven't much time."

Victor hated changing clothes in public. But he really hated changing into *girls'* clothes in public. As Victor had feared, these clearly belonged to Jaime. And they were several sizes too small.

He inched out from behind the tree.

"I can see your belly button," said Scott. "And your ankles. My mom has pants like that."

"I'm changing back," said Victor. "Where's Jaime?"

"She is already in position," said Franklin.

Victor took a step back. "What do you mean, she's 'in position'?"

Scott pointed to one of the suitcases, which looked considerably fuller than it had a moment before.

At least no one could see him in his ridiculous costume.

Still, Victor would have gladly traded places with Scott. Pulling a suitcase down the street was infinitely better than being pulled down the street *inside* a suitcase. Victor's knees were pressed up against his nose, and his foot was twisted at a painful angle. The air was growing hotter by the second, and he was finding it a little tough to breathe. He wondered how Jaime was faring.

Thud!

"Oops! Sorry, Jaime," whispered Scott. "Didn't see that hole."

Victor guessed that she was not faring well, either.

It seemed to take Franklin and Scott an unusually long time to find the entrance to the factory. More than once

Victor had to fight the urge to jump out and direct the situation. Finally, the ground beneath him became very smooth, and he guessed they had made it inside.

"Excuse me, ma'am," he heard Franklin say. "My nephew and I are from out of the town and we're a little lost. Can you help?"

"I'm sorry, sir, but this is private property." It was a woman's voice, very official. "Do you have business here?"

"We're looking for the bus station," said Scott.

"Just down the block to your right," said the woman. "Is that all?"

"I mean the train station," said Scott. "Where's that?"

"I'm afraid I'm going to have to ask you to leave," said the woman. "As I said, this is private—"

"My dad needs to sit down," said Scott. "Do you have anything to drink?"

"I am a bit parched," added Franklin.

"No, we don't have anything to drink. And I thought this man said he was your uncle."

"Uncle Dad, that's what I call him," said Scott.

Victor heard the sound of a button clicking. "Security?" said the woman. "I think we have a situation here in the lobby."

"A situation? Where?" said Franklin. Victor heard footsteps, and Franklin's voice grew softer. "Let's see if we can help!"

"They're probably bringing us drinks," said Scott. It

sounded like he was walking away too. "I hope they have root beer."

"Gentlemen," said the woman, "you're trespassing on private property. If you don't leave immediately, I'll call the police."

"The police! Maybe *they* could take us to the train station!" said Franklin.

"My feet hurt," said Scott. "I'm going to lie down for a minute to rest."

"Excellent idea!" said Franklin. "Wake us in a half hour, will you, ma'am?"

"Gentlemen, security is on its way!" Victor could hear the *clip-clop* of her footsteps as she followed Franklin and Scott.

"Now!" whispered Jaime.

Victor unzipped his suitcase and tumbled out onto the floor. Jaime climbed out of her suitcase beside him.

Franklin and Scott had chosen the perfect place to leave the bags. The main lobby of Infinity Unlimited was tall and open, but Victor and Jaime were safely hidden behind a row of large potted plants that decorated the edges.

Jaime gave Victor a nudge. She put her finger to her lips, then pointed toward a door behind the reception desk.

Victor nodded. Quickly, they zipped the suitcases back up.

In the distance, he could hear Franklin and Scott begin to sing "Yankee Doodle," the signal that the coast was clear.

SECRET SIGNAL SONGS AND WHAT THEY MEAN

"Yankee Doodle" .... The coast is clear.

"America the Beautiful" .... Danger—someone's coming.

"Happy Birthday to You". .... We've been spotted! Run for your life!

"Old MacDonald Had a Farm" .... Secret meeting tonight at headquarters.

"The Hokey Pokey". .... Enemy nearby. Be careful what you say.

"Mary Had a Little Lamb". .... Your fly is open.

"Twinkle, Twinkle, Little Star". .... I'm hungry. Let's stop for some tacos.

"London Bridge Is Falling Down"... Warning! London Bridge is falling down!

Jaime took off first, with Victor close at her heels. They kept low, following the row of plants for as far as they could. When they reached the end, they sprinted the final fifteen feet out in the open, then ducked behind the reception desk.

"Do you think anyone saw us?" panted Victor.

"I don't think so." For a moment, the two of them sat perfectly still, listening for any sign that they had been spotted. From the sound of things, the security guards had arrived to escort Franklin and Scott out of the building. To Victor's amazement, the plan was working.

"Ready?" said Jaime. She grabbed something from a shelf beneath the desk, then reached up for the doorknob.

"Hang on," said Victor. His heart was still racing. "I just need to catch my breath."

But Jaime was already gone.

CHAPTER TEN

Inside Infinity Unlimited

Victor hadn't expected it to look so ordinary.

Infinity Unlimited was just a big, busy office filled with cubicles. Men and women in business suits sat at computers, talking on phones and doing paperwork.

"Here, put this on," said Jaime. She slipped Victor a visitor's pass, then clipped one on her own shirt.

"Good thinking," said Victor. He glanced around the room. "What do we do next?"

Jaime started walking. "Act like you belong here. And keep an eye out for a door to the factory floor."

They passed rows and rows of desks. Most of the office workers were too busy to notice two kids passing by.

Occasionally, though, one would look up and smile at Victor's outfit.

"I can't believe you made me wear this," whispered Victor.

"Wait until we get inside the factory," said Jaime. "You'll thank me then. Remember, stick to the shadows."

At the end of the room, they found what they were looking for: a door with a sign that said AUTHORIZED PERSONNEL ONLY.

"You think this goes to the factory?" said Victor.

Jaime shrugged. "It goes *somewhere*. If it's the wrong door, we'll just pretend to be two kids who got lost. Be prepared, you might need to cry."

"Me? Why don't you do it?"

INFINITY UNLIMITED VISITOR'S PASS

VISITOR

Please return badge to front desk
3–A

INFINITY ∞ UNLIMITED

Benjamin Franklinstein Meets Thomas Deadison

"I don't cry," said Jaime matter-of-factly. "Besides, I'm wearing sunglasses."

She opened the door and they slipped inside.

It felt like stepping out into a bright, snowy winter day. *Everything* was white: the enormous walls, the floor, the strange machinery, even the workers' uniforms.

"Get down!" hissed Jaime. She tugged at his shirt.

Victor dropped to the floor beside her. They huddled behind a pair of white garbage cans, observing the factory in action. Just a few feet in front of them, conveyor belts delivered a never-ending stream of Infinity Bulbs to a line of workers. The workers boxed them and placed them on different belts, sending the bulbs farther down the line.

"We have to get out of here," said Jaime. "We'll be spotted any second."

"Definitely." Victor scanned the factory floor. Every inch of it glowed, as if they were inside an enormous lightbulb. "You know, I'm thinking maybe these black costumes weren't such—"

"Finish that sentence and I'll kill you."

"I'm just saying that—"

"Seriously. I will."

Victor pointed to a door about fifty feet down the wall, marked with a symbol of a staircase. "We could try that one."

"How?"

"In these." Victor reached up and very slowly tipped the

garbage can toward him. To his relief, it was nearly empty, except for a few papers. "We'll hide underneath and work our way along the wall. If we move slowly enough, they won't notice us."

"And if they do?"

"I'll cry," said Victor.

"Deal."

Victor tipped the garbage can over his head and ducked underneath. He could hear Jaime struggling with hers, then cursing. Evidently, her can was a little more full than his.

It took them ten minutes to cross the fifty feet to the door. Every time they heard footsteps approach, they froze, hoping that it wasn't a janitor. Then, once the foot-steps had safely passed, they would inch forward again. Finally, Victor felt the doorjamb.

"We're here."

Once through the door, Victor's eyes strained to adjust to the darkness of the stairwell. He could see that it went several stories above and below ground level.

"Up or down?" he asked.

"Do you hear that?" said Jaime.

Victor listened. A low hum was coming from somewhere deep beneath his feet. "Whatever's making that sound, it's pretty big."

"Exactly," said Jaime. "I say we head down and investigate."

With each set of stairs, the noise grew louder. Three floors down, they came to a thick, red metal door. Victor put his ear to it. The hum was strong now. He could feel it in his bones.

"If someone sees us, are we still two kids who got lost?"

"If someone sees us, we run," said Jaime. *"Fast."* She turned the knob and inched the door open a crack. Cautiously, they stepped through.

Victor had never seen such a big room. Perfectly round, its walls were taller than his house. Machines and computer panels with blinking lights lined the walls. All around, giant brass wheels spun beside twenty-foot coils that buzzed and sparked. And in the center of it all, a giant tower stretched upward through the high ceiling.

"What is it?" whispered Jaime.

"Some kind of giant antenna," whispered Victor. "The Emperor probably uses it to send his commands to the Infinity Bulbs."

"It's so big! I bet it runs straight up through the factory to the roof," said Jaime.

The tower stood on an island, separated from the rest of the room by a deep pit. Inside the pit, an enormous fan steadily spun like a merry-go-round. Its blades gave off a crackling blue glow. A narrow footbridge connected the island to the outer rim of the room where Jaime and Victor stood.

"Should we get a closer look?" whispered Jaime.

Victor nodded.

As they crept across the footbridge, Victor looked down at the blades whirring beneath him. The humming energy he had felt outside the door was strong now. A strange electrical breeze brushed across his skin.

"It's a huge electrical turbine," Jaime said. "This must be the main power plant."

"Yeah," said Victor. "I can feel the energy, and I'm not even touching it. Creepy."

Cautiously, they stepped onto the island at the center of the room. As they circled it, they could see scaffolding rising up the back side of the antenna.

"The Emperor hasn't quite finished it yet," whispered Victor, observing some loose cables hanging from above.

"And we can't let him finish," whispered Jaime. "How do we break it?"

"That's usually Scott's job." Victor studied the machinery. "But if we can sever the main power line—"

Jaime clapped a hand over Victor's mouth and pointed. On the far side of the room, four scientists in lab coats were fixing a machine. Jaime and Victor ducked around to the other side of the antenna and crept back across the bridge.

"I recognize them!" whispered Jaime. "They're Prometheans. They disappeared a month ago."

"The Emperor must be controlling them," said Victor. He hurried toward the red exit door. "He probably made them build all this stuff."

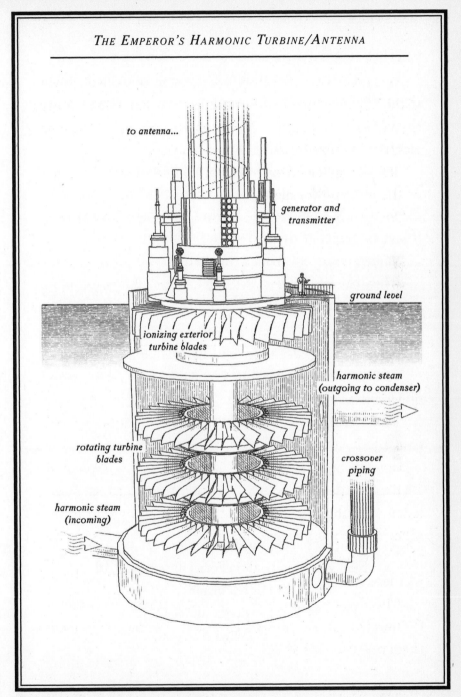

to antenna...

generator and
transmitter

ground level

ionizing exterior
turbine blades

harmonic steam
(outgoing to condenser)

rotating turbine
blades

crossover
piping

harmonic steam
(incoming)

"That makes sense," said Jaime. "I wonder if—"

The red exit door suddenly swung open in front of them. Two scientists—a man and a woman—stepped into the room.

There was nowhere to hide.

"Quick!" said Victor. "Let's try a different door."

He turned and began to run the other way. But when he glanced back, Jaime wasn't behind him. Instead she stood, frozen in place, as the two scientists approached her.

"Jaime, come on! What's the matter with you?"

"They're . . . they're . . ."

"Coming this way—I know!" He ran back to her. "Come on!"

"You don't understand," said Jaime.

"I understand we need to go," said Victor. Why wasn't she cooperating?

"Those people . . . they're *my parents*!"

THINGS SCOTT KNOWS HOW TO BREAK

Precisely calibrated scientific equipment
The washing machine
Skip Weaver's "Loudest Forecast" trophy, 2010
His left thumb
That thing at the museum
Wind

Benjamin Franklinstein Meets Thomas Deadison

CHAPTER ELEVEN
Family Reunion

Victor had no idea what to do.

"Mom! Dad! It's me, Jaime!"

Jaime's parents stopped and looked at her. Then, without warning, her mother reached out and grabbed her by the arms.

"Mom?" Jaime said, struggling. "What are you doing? You're hurting me!"

Her father took Victor by the wrist, dragged him to a console, and pressed a large button. Around the room, red lights flashed.

"Mom! Dad!" Jaime shrieked. "What's going on here?"

Victor struggled to break free. "Let go of me!" He lurched

forward and stomped down hard on Mr. Winters's foot. Mr. Winters cried out in pain and stumbled backward.

Victor ran to Jaime and yanked her free from her mother.

"They're under the Emperor's control," he said, leading Jaime toward the door.

"But I can help them!"

The shriek of a siren pierced the air.

"Jaime, they've sounded the alarm! *They're turning us in!*"

Like a splash of cold water, the noise shook her back to her senses. "You're right. Let's go."

Three flights up the stairwell, Jaime paused at the door to the factory floor. "We'll be spotted if we go back into the factory. Let's try that way instead."

They ran down a long cement hallway. By the time they reached the end, the sound of the alarms had faded. Victor listened at a door. "I hear beeping, like a truck backing up. I think we're at the rear of the building."

"That could be good." Jaime reached for the doorknob. "If we see an opening, we run for it, no looking back."

"Got it," said Victor. "And remember to stick to the shadows."

Jaime scowled, then eased the door open.

They were at the end of a loading area filled with row after row of large cardboard boxes, each marked with the Infinity Unlimited logo. At one end of the room, workers rapidly filled the boxes with lightbulbs from a conveyor belt. Just as quickly, the boxes were stacked on pallets, and at the other end, forklifts loaded the pallets onto trucks.

Victor and Jaime watched the operation for a moment, taking it all in.

"There are too many people," said Victor. "We'll be spotted for sure."

"Then we'll have to hide," said Jaime.

"Where?"

"There." She pointed to a stack of boxes sitting on a pallet. "The forklift is working its way down the line. In a few minutes, it will pick up that stack. We'll be inside."

"Yeah, and then we'll be trapped in a truck, driving to who-knows-where," said Victor. "How is that better?"

"You want to stay here? Come on."

Keeping low to the floor, they crawled over to the stack of boxes. Jaime pulled out a pocketknife and cut open a flap in the side of one of them. Then, as quickly as they could, she and Victor began to remove the Infinity Bulbs.

"We're going to be a lot heavier than a box of light-bulbs," said Victor.

"The forklift won't notice," said Jaime.

Victor climbed in first and tried to make himself as small as possible. Jaime squeezed in after him and pulled the flap shut.

"Let me borrow the knife for a second," whispered Victor.

"What for?"

"Airholes." Victor jabbed the knife into the bottom of the box, searching for gaps in the pallet below. Wherever he found one, he cut a small round vent.

"Good thinking," said Jaime.

"What now?"

"We wait."

It didn't take long. Soon Victor heard the sound of an engine approaching. He felt the pallet shake beneath them as they were lifted off the floor.

Through the small airholes, they watched the floor pass beneath them. They crossed the loading dock and were set down inside a truck. More pallets of boxes were stacked around and above them, and the light from the airholes grew dim. Finally, they heard the workers pull the door shut and the truck rumbled to life.

"I think we made it," whispered Jaime. "I'm going to call Dr. Franklin and let him know where we are." The light from her cell phone illuminated the inside of the box like a candle. "Hmm . . ."

"What's wrong?"

"All I hear is static."

Victor pulled out his own phone. "Me too. It's possible all these Infinity Bulbs are causing some kind of interference."

She turned off her phone and Victor did the same. For several minutes they rode on in silence.

"Can I ask you something?" said Victor.

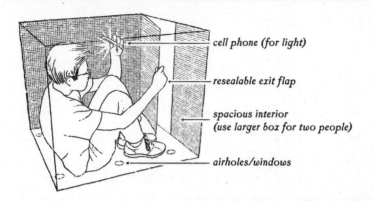

cell phone (for light)

resealable exit flap

spacious interior
(use larger box for two people)

airholes/windows

"Shoot."

"Even here in the dark, you're wearing your sunglasses. Isn't it hard to see?"

Jaime didn't respond. If he hadn't been sitting just inches away, Victor might have guessed she hadn't heard his question. "Sorry. It's none of my business."

"No, it's okay. It's just that . . . I don't usually talk about it. I've been wearing these sunglasses for months now, and it feels weird to take them off."

"How come? Are your eyes sensitive to light?"

"It's not that. Remember when I said I don't cry?"

"Yeah."

"Well, that's not exactly true."

Suddenly, it hit him. "Oh," Victor said softly.

There was a long silence, and then Jaime went on. "All my life, my parents have been training me to be strong, to be a Promethean. When they went missing, I had to help keep things going. It's been a lot to deal with."

"Why do *you* have to keep things going?"

"The Order is full of some of the smartest people you'll ever meet. Geniuses. But most of them have their heads in the clouds. There are a lot of things kids know about computers that grown-ups don't have a clue about. I help them with that stuff."

Victor thought about the times he had tried to teach his mom to text. "That can't be easy."

"It's impossible. Most of the time when they get stuck on something, I just end up doing it myself." She sighed. "Now, somehow, I'm in charge of the whole Promethean Underground communications network. I have to at least look like I have everything under control."

Victor shifted his body and tried to turn his foot, which had fallen asleep. "Is that your parents' specialty, communications?"

"No, electricity. They're engineers. They specialize in big stuff, like power plants and generators." Jaime sniffled. "Or at least they did."

"They're going to be okay."

"How do you know?"

"The Emperor needs them alive. Somehow, they're part of his plan."

"Is that supposed to make me feel better?"

"I guess so."

Jaime sighed. "I'll take it. Hey, listen to that."

The truck had stopped. Victor heard the back door open.

There was a scraping sound above them. Someone was removing the box directly over their heads.

Jaime pulled the side flap open. "We're blocked in over here," she hissed. "All right, new plan. We're probably at some supermarket or something. As soon as they open the box to investigate, we'll jump up and catch them by surprise. If they grab us, we'll scream like we're being kidnapped."

Victor felt their pallet being dragged across the floor and then lifted up into the air. He could see a man's feet through the airholes.

Incredibly, the man was carrying them away!

"There's no way this guy thinks we're lightbulbs," Victor whispered.

"Shhh!" Jaime hissed. "Just get ready to run."

Victor watched the floor as they were carried down the ramp from the truck, across a long room, and into an elevator. The elevator descended, the door opened, and they went down a long hallway. They passed through a second doorway and entered a carpeted room. The man placed the pallet on the floor, as gently as someone would set a baby into a crib.

With one quick motion, the top of the box was ripped away. Victor tensed, ready to jump. He never got the chance. A blinding light beamed down into his eyes.

CHAPTER TWELVE
The Emperor Revealed

"Don't bother trying to hypnotize them, Thomas. Your power will not work on them, although I am not sure why." The voice was old and had a foreign accent.

"As you wish."

The light dimmed. Victor's vision was dappled with a kaleidoscope of color. Through the spots he could just make out the figure of a man staring down at him.

"Help!" Victor screamed. "Help! We're being kidnapped!"

Dark laughter echoed through the room.

"Don't bother," said Jaime. "We're not at a supermarket."

She was right. As Victor's eyes adjusted, he began to make out details of the room and the man standing above him—Thomas Edison!

"Shall I remove them from the box?" asked Edison.

"I'm sure that won't be necessary," said the other man. "Children, won't you please come out and join us?"

Victor looked at Jaime. She nodded back. Cautiously, they stood up and stepped out of the box.

They were in a lavish study, lined with scarlet velvet wallpaper and heavy curtains. Large oil paintings hung along one wall, on either side of a heavy door. To the right, antique bookshelves alternated with marble sculptures on dark wooden pedestals. An enormous globe, as tall as a tractor tire, stood in the center.

It was all so unexpected that it took Victor a moment to notice the bizarre spectacle behind him.

Hundreds of monitors were mounted on the back wall, spanning the entire length of the room. They showed a constant stream of video. On them, Victor could see office workers, city streets, and even the insides of people's homes. Several monitors focused on the Infinity Unlimited factory itself, including the loading dock.

Victor realized that they had been watched the entire time.

Across the room, a small, wrinkled man sat in what appeared to be an oversize antique bathtub. He wore a large, curved hat and an old-fashioned military jacket. The top of his tub was covered so it formed a desk. On the desk sat a pile of papers and what looked like a large remote control.

The bottom of the tub stood on four short legs, each ending with a foot shaped like a lion's paw. Victor had seen bathtubs like that in movies and old photographs.

But these legs were moving.

Clunk-clunk, clunk-clunk, clunk-clunk.

"Welcome to my home," said the man. The bathtub rocked ever so slightly from side to side as the short mechanical legs carried him forward. "You must be Victor, and of course I recognize Jaime Winters. You, my dear, are the spitting image of your mother."

The man smiled as he spoke, but there was nothing friendly about his tone. Jaime scowled at him.

"I assume you already know my assistant, Thomas Alva Edison?"

Edison nodded.

Victor concentrated on the withered old man in the bathtub. There was something oddly familiar about him.

"So who does that make you?" said Jaime, her voice cool and calm. Victor had to admit, the sunglasses were great for hiding emotion.

"You may call me the Emperor," said the little old man. He tipped his hat in her direction.

The hat.

The accent.

The Emperor.

"You're Napoléon Bonaparte!" gasped Victor. "Emperor of France. One of the greatest generals in history."

The old man raised an eyebrow. "*One of* the greatest?"

"But . . . ," Jaime stammered. "But you're . . ."

"Dead?" said Napoléon with a chuckle. "Surely you of all people should realize that death does not always mean the end."

"That bathtub you're in," Victor said. "It's a Leyden casket, isn't it?"

"*Mais oui!*" the Emperor answered. "You are correct. I live forever, thanks to the Order!"

"But the Modern Order of Prometheus only preserves inventors," said Jaime. "*You're* not an inventor."

"True, true," said Napoléon. "I suppose I am the only member who does not have that distinction. Now, we need to get the two of you to your quarters. Thomas?"

Edison walked across the room and pulled open a pair of curtains, revealing a door made of metal bars. Behind the door was a small cell. He pulled out a key, unlocked the door, and motioned for Jaime and Victor to step inside.

"I would not attempt escape, if I were you," said Napoléon. "The preservation process has transformed Mr. Edison, giving him remarkable power. He will be happy to demonstrate it, should the need arise."

Edison took a step forward, and Jaime stumbled back into the cardboard box, onto her back. "Don't touch me!" she shouted. She struggled to stand, but her foot slipped and she fell again, ripping the box.

"Now, now," Napoléon muttered, "there is no need for

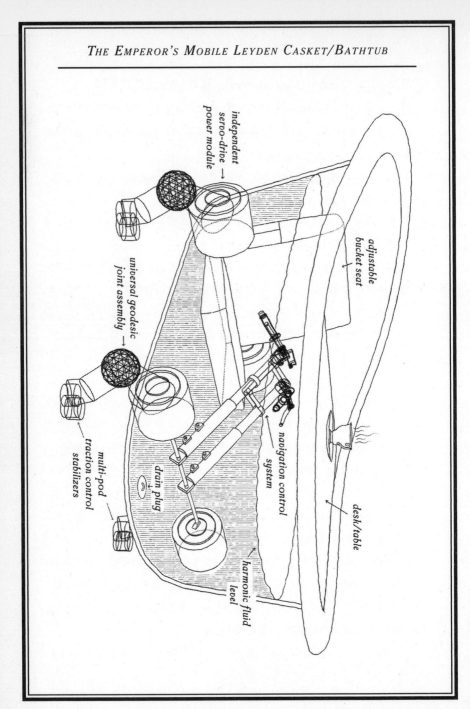

independent servo-drive power module

adjustable bucket seat

universal geodesic joint assembly

navigation control system

multi-pod traction control stabilizers

drain plug

desk/table

harmonic fluid level

panic. He will not hurt you . . . so long as you do as I ask."

"Shall I carry them, my Emperor?" asked Edison.

"That's their choice. Children?"

Edison took another step toward Jaime. "We'll walk," she said with a sigh.

Jaime stood up and followed Victor into the cell. As Edison began to shut the door, she blocked it with her hands and called out to Napoléon. "How long are you going to keep us here?"

"Not long," he answered. "A day at the most."

Jaime stepped forward, but Edison pushed her back. She tumbled to the floor of the cell. The door slammed shut.

OTHER INVENTORS PRESERVED BY THE ORDER

Inventor and Year Preserved	*Invention*
1799 - Jacques Montgolfiere	Hot air balloon
1810 - Joseph Montgolfiere	Hot air balloon
1848 - George Stephenson	Steam Locomotive
1852 - Countess Ada Lovelace	Computer programming
1871 - Charles Babbage	Mechanical Computer
1872 - Samuel Morse	Electric Telegraph
1896 - Alfred Nobel	Dynamite
1943 - George Washington Carver	300 uses for peanuts
1943 - Nikola Tesla	Tesla Coil
1953 - Mary Anderson	Windshield Wiper
1985 - James Alexander Dewar	The Twinkie

CHAPTER THIRTEEN
Trapped!

For the next hour, there was nothing for Victor and Jaime to do but watch as Napoléon went about his business. People came and went, receiving orders from the little man in the bathtub. Jaime recognized a number of them as missing Custodians of the Order.

"Hey, it's Ms. Aldini!" Jaime exclaimed. "Help!"

Ms. Aldini turned her head slowly and looked at Jaime and Victor. Then she turned back and continued with her work. She left the room with papers in her hands.

"I don't think she even recognized us," Jaime said. "Did you see the look on her face?"

"Blank, just like the looks on your parents' faces," Victor said. "Hey, I wonder if our phones work now."

"I already checked. Still blocked."

A clock chimed, and the Emperor abruptly ordered everyone but Edison to leave the room.

"Bring me the microphone," said Napoléon. "It is time for another broadcast."

Edison walked over to a tall cabinet and opened it. It was filled with knobs, gauges, and bulbs, all glowing different colors. He picked up a wireless microphone and delivered it to the Emperor's tiny, gnarled hand.

"Alert the factory and tell them to warm up the harmonic supertransmitter," said Napoléon.

Edison typed at a keyboard. Several minutes passed, and then a light on the cabinet turned from red to green. Edison looked up and nodded.

The Emperor took a deep breath, placed the microphone to his lips, and spoke in a soothing voice.

"Listen to me."

The colored lights pulsated and the voice echoed inside Victor's brain.

"I can hear his voice in my head," said Victor. "It's louder and clearer than ever. You're sure you can't hear it?"

"No," said Jaime. "Just his whispering from over there."

"Relax and prepare for your orders."

On the wall of screens, people all throughout Philadelphia paused and stared off into space. "He's hypnotizing the entire city!" said Jaime.

"See that monitor showing the library?" said Victor.

"Watch the lights near the door the next time he says something."

"Focus your mind."

"I saw it!" whispered Jaime. "They got brighter for a second."

"It's definitely the Infinity Bulbs," said Victor. "He's using light to broadcast his messages. Now everyone in the city can hear his commands."

"Except me," said Jaime. "How come I haven't been hypnotized?"

Victor studied Jaime's face. "You never take off those sunglasses, do you?"

"Never."

"That's why! Your sunglasses block the light from the Infinity Bulbs."

"But lots of people wear sunglasses," said Jaime. "And everybody turns off the lights at night when they go to sleep. So how come they're hypnotized?"

"Maybe it has to build up over time," said Victor. "For example, I'm allergic to cats. After I got my first allergy shot, I didn't notice any difference. I had to go back again and again for more shots before I stopped sneezing all the time. The point is, it took a while for the treatment to work."

"So since my eyes are never directly exposed to the light . . ."

". . . the hypnotic effect never gets a chance to build up."

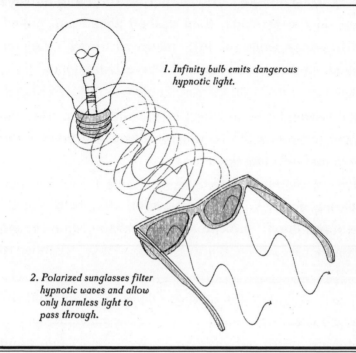

1. Infinity bulb emits dangerous hypnotic light.

2. Polarized sunglasses filter hypnotic waves and allow only harmless light to pass through.

Jaime adjusted her sunglasses and let out a low whistle. "Wow."

Across the room, Napoléon was concluding his broadcast.

"You will be contacted soon with important instructions," he continued. *"You may now return to your lives."* He slumped against the back of his tub and motioned for Edison. The microphone fell to the floor beside him. "I'm suddenly tired, Thomas. Please walk with me to my chambers."

The tub turned and trudged across the room. Edison turned off the machine, then dashed ahead and pulled open the door. Once the little man was through, Edison followed, shutting and locking the door behind him.

"I have an idea," said Victor. "If only we could get to that microphone."

"Who says we can't?" said Jaime. She gave the cell door a shove and it swung open.

Victor was speechless.

"It's an old trick," said Jaime, motioning to the latch plate in the door. "Remember when Edison came at me? I pretended to fall back into the box. Then I grabbed a

HOW TO JAM A LOCK WITH PAPER

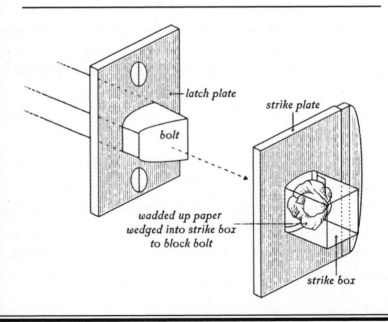

latch plate

bolt

strike plate

wadded up paper
wedged into strike box
to block bolt

strike box

little piece of cardboard. Just before he closed us in here, I jammed the lock with it."

"So, this whole time . . ."

". . . it was open," said Jaime. She stepped out of the cell and into the room. "I didn't dare say anything until the coast was clear. So what's your plan?"

Victor ran to the wooden cabinet. "If we can figure out how this thing works, we can contact Ben and Scott." He studied the console, looking for the power switch.

"How?"

"Remember, they hear Napoléon's voice inside their heads too. If I can get this microphone to work, I can tell them where we are." Victor flipped a switch and the console lit up.

"But won't all of Philadelphia hear your message too?"

Victor shook his head. "Remember, everyone else in the city only gets Napoléon's messages *subconsciously.* They don't hear the actual words." He ran to where the microphone lay in the middle of the room, picked it up, then stopped short. "Oh no!"

"What?"

"How can we tell them where we are if *we* don't know where we are?"

But Jaime didn't respond. She was looking past Victor.

Edison and Napoléon were at the door.

"You are at Seventeen Parker Avenue," said Napoléon with a sly smile. "Please tell your friends to come at once."

CHAPTER FOURTEEN
The Emperor's Plan

"But before you call your friends," said Napoléon, "I want you to see something." He picked up the remote control and aimed it at the monitors. Instantly, an image of Jaime's parents filled the wall. They stood beside a console at the base of the supertransmitter. Behind them, Victor could see the blades of the turbine spinning in the pit.

"I'm sure you recognize this lovely couple," said Napoléon.

Jaime glared at the Emperor.

"As you can see, your parents are under my control. When my master plan is complete, I will have no further use for them. If you cooperate, you have my word that they will be released unharmed. If not, well, we may have to consider less pleasant options."

Victor noticed Jaime's lip begin to quiver.

"So here is what you will do," continued Napoléon. "Send your message as planned to Dr. Franklin and his friends, and tell them to come at once."

"Never," said Jaime. "We'd be leading them straight into a trap."

"That is true. But consider the alternative. Thomas, hand me the microphone."

Edison took the microphone from Victor and gave it to the Emperor.

"Now watch." Napoléon motioned to the screen. *"Mr. and Mrs. Winters, please take one step toward the turbine."*

The camera followed Jaime's parents as they stepped toward the pit. The whirring blades spun just a few feet beneath them.

"Take another step forward and open the safety gate."

Mr. and Mrs. Winters were now balanced at the pit's edge.

"Tell me, Jaime. Would you prefer I command them to plunge *into* the spinning turbine? Or is your friend Victor going to do as I ask?"

"All right," said Victor. "We'll do what you want."

"But Victor—"

"He'll kill your parents, Jaime. I know it." Victor turned to Edison. "Give me the microphone."

"Very good," said Napoléon. "Simply tell Dr. Franklin that you have found an important clue and that he should come at once."

"Don't do it," urged Jaime. "He's bluffing. Somehow, he needs my parents for his plan. Otherwise, he wouldn't have taken them in the first place."

Victor glanced up at the screen. "What was the address again?"

"Seventeen Parker Avenue," said Napoléon.

Victor nodded and put the microphone to his lips. "Ben, Scott—this is Victor. Everything's fine. We've found something important. Come at once to Seventeen Parker Avenue. That's *Parker*, not *Barker*, spelled with a *P* as in *part*, not a *B* as in *backward*."

His hand trembled as he handed the microphone back to Edison.

"Very well done," said Napoléon. "Now please step back into your cell."

The next hour was excruciating. All Victor could do was watch and wait and hope that Ben understood his message. Whatever the Emperor was planning, it was clearly going to happen soon. More and more people came into the room to receive orders, and at one point Napoléon dispatched Edison on some sort of urgent mission.

Jaime sat fuming in the back of the cell. She hadn't said

a word to Victor since he had sent the message. Victor understood her anger, but he didn't dare tell her what his message had actually said. Not yet.

A buzzer sounded, and Napoléon turned his attention to one of the monitors. It showed a parking lot from high above. On the screen he saw Franklin and Scott strolling between the cars. They approached a metal door at the back of a large brick building. Franklin opened the door and they stepped inside. From the console, another buzzer sounded.

"What are they doing?" Victor whispered. "They were supposed to sneak in."

"How were they supposed to know?" grumbled Jaime from the back of the cell. "You told them everything was fine."

Napoléon pressed another button and the entire wall filled with the image of Franklin and Scott walking down a long hallway.

Suddenly, uniformed guards approached from behind. As Franklin turned to look, more guards emerged from the front. They were trapped.

"NO!" shouted Jaime.

A guard pressed a small handheld device to one of Franklin's neck bolts. There was a flash and the old man fell to the floor. Another guard grabbed Scott from behind. Napoléon switched off the video feed and the screens returned to images of the city.

Jaime rattled the cell door and screamed. "You animal! When the Modern Order of Prometheus discovers where you are, you'll pay for this!"

Napoléon turned his bathtub to face Jaime. "But my dear," he said, chuckling, "I *am* the Modern Order of Prometheus. Haven't you figured that out by now? And the way you shake your cage, *you* seem more like the animal to me."

Jaime rattled the metal door again, banging and kicking. "You're a monster!" she screamed.

"Jaime," said Victor. "That's not going to help."

She spun toward him. "Shut up!" She sobbed. "I told you not to send the message! Now they're . . . they're . . ."

"They're here," said Victor. "Look."

Several guards carried Franklin through the door. Two others restrained Scott, who was struggling to break free. Edison followed behind.

"Very good, Thomas," said Napoléon. "Please put them with the others."

Edison walked to the cell and unlocked the thick metal door. He glared at Victor and Jaime, his message clear: Any attempt to escape would be punished.

The guards carried Franklin to the edge of the cell and pushed him inside. Victor and Jaime caught his head just before it hit the floor. Another guard shoved Scott through the door and slammed it shut.

"Are you all right?" said Victor.

"We got your message," said Scott.

"But I—"

"We got your message," repeated Scott, with a wink.

Jaime looked at Scott, then Victor, curiously. Behind her, Franklin was beginning to stir. She knelt down beside him.

"Dr. Franklin, can you hear me?"

Slowly, Franklin sat up and shook his head, as if trying to clear water from his ear. "I'm fine, Jaime. Just a little shaken up."

There was a clattering noise as Napoléon piloted his bathtub over to the cell. He cleared his throat, and the prisoners turned toward him.

"I am sorry for the unpleasant welcome, Dr. Franklin. My name is Napoléon Bonaparte, Emperor of France and, soon, the world. Please forgive me for tricking you into coming."

"Tricks and treachery are the practice of fools," said Franklin.

The Emperor's face grew serious. "If any other person spoke to me as you just did, I would have him killed." He paused and took a deep breath. "But you are the great Benjamin Franklin, and I am the great Napoléon Bonaparte. I hope that we can work together once my business with the people of Philadelphia is complete."

"And what business is that?" asked Franklin.

"The business of creating a better world, of course!" Napoléon answered. "I attempted this in my first life. I had

Napoléon Bonaparte
Emperor

Objective

To create—and rule—a perfect world.

Background

Born Napoleone di Buonaparte in Corsica, 15 August 1769

5' 7" tall.

Embodies the ambitions of thirty million Frenchmen.

Education

École Militaire in Paris (1784–1785)

Military Academy at Brienne-le-Château (1779–1784)

Mme. Pamplemousse's Kindergarten for Bossy Children (1774–1775)

Accomplishments

Emperor of France (1799–1814)

Invaded Egypt. Very hot.

Invaded Russia. Very cold.

Took second place at the Battle of Waterloo.

Inspired a pastry.

Infiltrated and took command of the Modern Order of Prometheus.

Hobbies

Leading coups.

Plotting.

World travel and conquest.

Extended island vacations.

Hypnosis.

Keeping several steps ahead of my opponents.

wonderful ideas, ideas that would make the world great. And a strong army to spread those ideas!"

He sighed. "But people are complicated. They never understood my genius. I was thrown in prison! Me—the Emperor! But now I have a second chance. Here in Philadelphia, where the Modern Order of Prometheus was born, I can awaken any scientist to invent what I need. Mr. Edison's supertransmitter will be ready within the hour. Then I shall make the people understand. I . . . no, *we* will do their thinking for them, Dr. Franklin. If you will join me, we can change the world. With your help, Utopia beckons!"

"The devil sweetens poison with honey," Franklin scoffed.

"We shall see how you feel after all is done." Napoléon glanced at the grandfather clock in the corner. "But now, it is time to return to the factory and set our plan into motion."

Napoléon and Edison started for the door. The Emperor paused and looked back, a smile on his face. "The next time you see me, Philadelphia will be mine."

CHAPTER FIFTEEN
Breaking Out

Victor rattled the bars, but the door wouldn't budge. "Ben, why didn't you and Scott sneak in? When I sent that message, I was very clear that this was a trap."

"What are you talking about?" Jaime interrupted. "You didn't say anything to them about a trap."

Franklin smiled. "Ah, but Jaime, Victor did let me know that it was a trap."

Jaime looked puzzled.

"Yeah," Scott said. "Victor said that the address was on Parker Avenue, not Barker Avenue: *P* as in *part,* not *B* as in *backward.* I thought Victor was just being helpful because I sometimes get confused about directions and stuff. But Ben figured out that it was a hidden message."

"*Part* spelled backward is *trap*," Franklin explained. "Well communicated, Victor. And right under the Emperor's nose!"

"So why didn't you tell me you'd sent a secret message?" Jaime said.

"Why didn't you tell me that the cell door wasn't really locked?"

"Because if I told you, Napoléon and Edison would have . . . ," Jaime began. "Oh, right. Sorry, Victor."

"It's okay," Victor said. "Actually, when you got mad at me, it made the whole thing more convincing. But it still doesn't change the fact that we're all trapped."

"Far from it, my boy," Franklin said. "Let me show you what the Promethean Underground created for me. After I shorted out during our adventure at the pond, they rebuilt my battery belt—with some clever improvements."

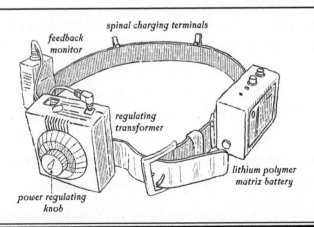

THE FRANKLIN BATTERY BELT VERSION 2.0

spinal charging terminals

feedback monitor

regulating transformer

lithium polymer matrix battery

power regulating knob

Franklin showed them a black metallic box attached to his belt. At the center was a red knob with a small pointer. A gauge circled the knob—blue at one end and red at the other.

"Impressive," Victor said. "And this belt is a lot smaller than the last one."

"The knob allows me to regulate the amount of power flowing through my body. If I need to rest and recharge, I turn it down to the blue zone. But if I need an extra burst of strength, I can turn it up."

Victor was skeptical. "But if it goes up into the red zone, couldn't you lose control?"

"I don't want that to happen again," Scott said. "Remember that time back at Ernie's Hardware when you threw a bathtub at us?"

"That will not happen," Franklin said. "The red zone is the upper limit of power I can reach *without* losing control. The knob will not turn any farther. The engineers call it a fail-safe. Watch."

Franklin took a few deep breaths and then slowly turned the knob into the red zone.

Victor watched Franklin for any signs of trouble. The old man's eyes glowed red, but only slightly. "Ben?"

"I'm *fine*, Victor. Now if you will please step out of the way."

Victor backed away from the door. Franklin grasped two bars and pulled. They wavered, bent, and then snapped from their frame. Franklin dropped them and proceeded to tear two more from the door, leaving a gap large enough for them to escape.

"Awesome!" Scott exclaimed. "Let's get out of here!"

"A moment, please." Franklin slumped to the floor, weary. "I need to recharge. This may take a while."

He turned the knob down to the blue zone and closed his eyes.

MEANWHILE . . .

"How much longer?" Napoléon demanded.

Edison stood at the base of the harmonic supertransmitter, staring into an open panel filled with dozens of loose wires. "I will finish it quickly, my Emperor. But first we must power down the dynamo."

"No, it must remain on at all times," Napoléon said. "The plan requires it."

"The supertransmitter is very close to losing its harmonic field. I have to rewire these circuits as quickly as possible, but I can't do it if the dynamo is running. The surge of power could kill me."

The Emperor pondered the problem. Turning off the power for only a moment would not affect his control over normal people. But Edison was not normal. His veins coursed with harmonic fluid. Cutting the electrical connection for even a few seconds might allow Edison to break the spell.

Yet only Edison had the knowledge and skill to complete the challenging operation. The Emperor had to risk it. "Very well." He nodded to Mr. and Mrs. Winters. They pushed a combination of buttons and twisted a dial on the console in front of them. The blades of the turbine whirred to a halt.

"Now, Thomas—*quickly*!"

Edison began twisting wires together. Napoléon marveled at the speed and accuracy with which the inventor attached them.

But halfway through his task, Edison slowed and then stopped. He looked at the wires he held between his fingers. "This doesn't . . . feel . . . right."

"You dare defy my direct order?" Napoléon growled. "Finish it now!"

"No, this . . . this is wrong," Edison stammered. "This machine . . . it's evil!" He let go of the wires and turned to Napoléon, puzzled. "What am I doing here? Who . . . who are you?"

"Turn the power back on!" Napoléon screamed at Jaime's parents. "Now!"

Mr. Winters pressed some buttons on the console and Mrs. Winters twisted the dial. The dynamo clacked, hummed, and began spinning again. The low whir quickly built to a high-pitched whine. Edison stiffened and a blankness overcame his eyes.

"Complete your work, Thomas," Napoléon said. "I command you!"

Edison grasped the wires again and continued joining them, his deft fingers a blur. Electricity sparked through his body. His hair stood on end, and he glowed a blinding white. Napoléon turned away, shielding his eyes.

"My Emperor!" Mrs. Winters called. "The harmonic field is in jeopardy! We have only seconds!"

"Finish it!" Napoléon screamed. "Now!"

A moment later, Edison pulled his hands away from the wires. His white glow dimmed to yellow, then orange, and finally disappeared completely. "It is complete, my Emperor."

Napoléon looked to the Winterses for confirmation.

"It's working," Mr. Winters said. "The harmonic field is intact."

Napoléon smiled. "Arise, Thomas, and cast your eyes upon your greatest invention."

Edison staggered to his feet and gazed at the awe-inspiring machine.

"The harmonic supertransmitter!" Napoléon declared. "Your incredible invention has strengthened my hypnotic control a thousandfold. Now I have complete control over everyone in the city. Today Philadelphia, tomorrow the world!"

CHAPTER SIXTEEN
Escape into Danger!

Franklin lay still on the cell floor. Jaime hovered over him, watching for signs of movement. "It's been nearly half an hour."

"He told us it might take a while for his batteries to recharge," Victor said from the other side of the room.

Victor and Scott had been using the time to explore. Scott pointed to a blinking group of ten monitors. "Look at all those Infinity Unlimited trucks."

"He's got them parked all over Philadelphia," Victor said. "He must be planning to ship the bulbs to other cities."

"I'm waking Dr. Franklin," Jaime said. "We're running out of time."

"Just give him another minute," Victor said, looking

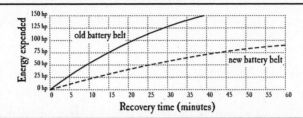

away from the screens. "I'm sure he'll be—"

"I awaken!" Franklin shouted, bolting upright.

Victor, Scott, and Jaime jumped in surprise.

"How long have I been recharging?" Franklin asked.

"About thirty minutes," Jaime said.

"Then we have no time to waste! Let us find an exit."

The four dashed across the room to a door, and Jaime threw it open. They could see an elevator and a staircase at the end of a long hall.

Jaime raced ahead and up the stairs. "Over here! I found a way out."

Victor, Scott, and Franklin began climbing the staircase but were suddenly stopped by a piercing voice in their heads.

"Attention! Citizens of Philadelphia, stop what you are doing. You are now under full command of the Emperor. Prepare for instructions."

Victor howled, holding his head. Franklin fell to his knees. Scott squeezed his eyes shut and put his fingers in his ears.

"What's wrong?" Jaime asked.

"It's Napoléon!" Victor shouted. "But his voice! It's so much louder than before!"

"Go immediately to any one of the ten redistribution centers throughout the city and load Infinity Bulbs onto our trucks. If you see anyone not following orders, carry them to a tanning salon for behavior correction."

The noise stopped. Victor, Ben, and Scott tried to clear their heads.

"What did he say?" Jaime asked.

"He told everyone to load Infinity Bulbs onto his trucks," Scott said.

"Then Victor was right," Jaime said.

"Yes. The Emperor is expanding his control beyond Philadelphia," Franklin confirmed. "The world is in imminent danger."

Jaime peered outside the door. "Speaking of danger, we've got another problem. Take a look."

Victor, Franklin, and Scott stumbled up the stairs and peeked out the door.

Cars sat abandoned on the streets, their doors left open. Hundreds of people trudged slowly forward, their eyes rolling back in their heads. They moved like parts of a great machine. Some groups headed east, some north, but all of them moved with purpose. They were following orders.

"They're zombies!" Scott cried.

CHAPTER SEVENTEEN
Zombies, Zombies Everywhere

"We need a plan," Jaime said. "Ideas?"

Franklin gazed upon the sea of people. "Look at them—the vacant expressions upon their faces. The Emperor has stolen their free will. Horrible!"

A scream slashed through the silence. Across the street, a woman in sunglasses struggled against four snarling zombies. They clutched her by the arms and legs. Dozens more surrounded her. The woman was lifted up on top of the group and carried down the street, screaming.

"They must be taking her to a tanning salon," Scott said.

"Why a tanning salon?" Jaime asked.

Scott shrugged. "Beats me."

"Those were Napoléon's orders," Victor explained. "He

said they needed *behavior correction*. My guess is that they've installed supercharged Infinity Bulbs into the tanning beds."

Jaime shivered. "We've got to stop them!" She took a step out of the doorway, but Franklin pulled her back.

"No," he said. "There are too many."

Victor studied the legions of spellbound Philadelphians. "I have an idea. Take a good look at them: their sluggish movements, the empty expressions on their faces, their lack of speech."

"That's what zombies do," Scott said.

"But look closer," Victor continued. "They only grab people who act differently from them, like that lady. They leave one another alone."

"I get it!" Scott said. "We need to be zombies, too."

"It's brilliant!" agreed Franklin. "Now all we have to do is figure out where to go."

"There's only one place we can go," Jaime said. "Infinity Unlimited. We have to break into the factory and destroy the supertransmitter."

Suddenly, Scott looked worried. "I just thought of something. If everyone has turned into zombies, then my mom is a zombie. Your mom, too, Victor. Everyone from school. All our friends . . ."

Victor felt sick. "I hadn't thought of that."

The four of them silently plodded along North 5th Street, their faces empty. They passed a souvenir shop and Victor stopped. "Wait for me. I've got to get something."

He ducked into the store and reappeared half a minute later wearing a knapsack.

"What did you get that for?" Jaime asked.

"I filled it with sunglasses," Victor said. "They might come in handy later."

They continued to trudge until Scott stopped in front of the open door of an empty barbershop. He stood there, transfixed. "Hey, guys?"

Jaime, Victor, and Franklin slowly lumbered back to Scott. "Come on," Victor urged in his best zombie voice. "Do you want to get caught?"

Scott pointed at a television mounted on the wall. "Look."

Scott's dad, Skip Weaver, was on the television screen, the image slightly off-kilter. He stood in front of the WURP Action News desk, waving his arms and screaming: *". . . and if anyone from the Promethean Underground is listening, I need help! I'm trapped up here. People of Philadelphia! Lock your doors and board up your windows! They've overrun the city! They're after you . . . they're after all of us!"*

Suddenly, there was a crunching noise from off camera. Skip snapped his head to the side in terror: *"They're here already! You're next! You're next!"*

Skip fled off screen. Seconds later, a slow-moving mob of zombies trudged from the right side of the room to the left. There was a crash and a scream. Then the screen went black.

"They got my dad," Scott whispered.

Victor tried to put a hand on his shoulder, but Scott shrugged it off angrily. "THEY GOT MY DAD!"

Jaime whipped around. Dozens of zombies turned and glared at them. "Scott, they heard you!"

It was too late. A hundred zombies turned to face them. Slowly, they began to shuffle forward. Rage and menace filled their faces.

"Scott," Victor said urgently, "they're coming."

"Master Weaver," Franklin said, "your father may yet be safe. But we shall never know for certain unless we leave at once."

Scott blinked at the screen, and then turned around to see the horde closing in. He wiped his eyes with the back of his hand. "Let's get out of here."

They took off, running down the street. Fortunately, the zombies moved slowly. Unfortunately, there were hundreds of them. And each time Victor glanced back, fifty more had joined the mob.

Jaime led the way. They raced around the corner onto Chestnut Street and skidded to a halt. Hundreds of zombies were approaching from the other end of the street.

"Uh-oh," Scott said.

The pack behind them continued to grow. Even more shambled in from the sides.

"They're closing in!" Jaime said. "We need to lose them."

"I know where we can hide," Franklin said. He led them halfway down the block and around an old building.

"Independence Hall!" Victor said.

"Exactly. Of course in my day, we called it the Pennsylvania State House, but once we signed the—"

Jaime pushed open the door. "Come on, before they see us!"

The four dashed into the building and stopped to catch their breath.

"What do we do now?" Victor whispered.

"We wait," Jaime said. "Sooner or later they'll stop looking for us and move on. Then we'll go back outside and pretend to be zombies again."

"How long do you think that will take?" Scott asked.

Victor shrugged. For several long minutes, the four of them stood in perfect silence.

Franklin cupped a hand to his ear. "Did you hear that?" he whispered.

Victor heard a shuffling sound just outside the door.

"Is that a squirrel?" Scott whispered. "I hope it's a squirrel."

BAM!

Suddenly, from all sides, doors flew open and zombies began streaming into the building.

"Follow me!" Franklin led Victor, Scott, and Jaime up a staircase. The mob began climbing after them.

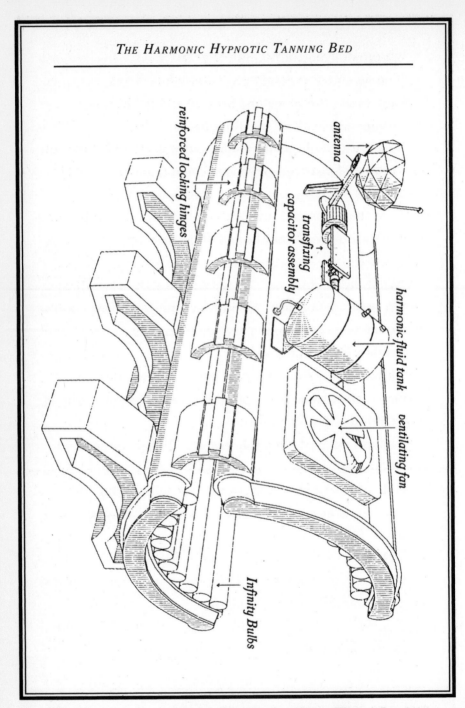

Benjamin Franklinstein Meets Thomas Deadison

"Where do we go now?" Scott asked.

"The only place we can go," Jaime said. "Up!"

They kept climbing until they reached the top of the final staircase. "Now what?" Victor asked.

"That ladder!" Franklin said, pointing. He led them up the rungs and pushed open a trapdoor in the ceiling. "This is the bell tower."

Once they were all inside, Jaime closed the trapdoor. Together, they pushed a tall, heavy crate over the top of it, blocking the entrance.

"Good lord!" Franklin said, peering outside the tower. Victor, Scott, and Jaime joined him and looked down. Independence Hall was surrounded.

Beneath them, hundreds of zombies were forming human pyramids, climbing over one another and up the sides of the building. The crate rattled as fists pounded on the trapdoor from below.

"They're here!" Scott said.

A Comparison of Zombies and Squirrels

SQUIRRELS	ZOMBIES
Scamper playfully	Stumble creepily
Soft and furry	Rotting and scaly
Alive	Undead
Eat nuts	Eat brains

Source: International Institute for Squirrel and Zombie Studies

CHAPTER EIGHTEEN
Trapped in the Tower

Victor's face went ashen. "They'll never give up. We're done for."

"Maybe not," Scott said, pointing at the sky. "Look!"

A small shape, silhouetted against the clouds, was growing larger. "A gyroplane!"

"Help!" Jaime called, waving her arms frantically. "Over here!"

The gyroplane banked to the left and began to fly away.

"He can't see us!" Victor said.

"I have an idea," Scott said. He climbed onto the crate, jumped, and grabbed the bell rope. With a deafening din, the Centennial Bell began to clang.

The gyroplane tipped back and began to head toward Independence Hall.

"Look!" Jaime said. "He heard it!"

But Victor was too distracted to notice. A hand appeared outside the window next to him, followed by another. The pyramid of zombies had reached the top!

"It's too late," Scott cried.

"Maybe not," Franklin said. "I'm going to buy you some time."

"What do you mean?" Victor asked.

Franklin gave Victor a grim look. "No matter what happens, promise that you will not try to follow me."

He reached for his battery belt and turned the knob all the way up to the farthest edge of the red zone. Then he gave the knob an extra twitch. It snapped and twisted some more.

Franklin's eyes burned bright red, and he let out a bloodcurdling howl. He leapt through the window and dove onto the roof below. As he fell, he took the tower of zombies down with him. Franklin disappeared into the swarming mass.

Jaime screamed. "Dr. Franklin . . . no!"

Franklin emerged from the crowd and began pulling more climbers down, tossing them away from the bell tower.

"He supercharged himself!" Scott said.

"There are too many of them," Jaime said. "He'll be killed!"

There was a rush of wind as the gyroplane descended from the clouds and hovered above Independence Hall. A rope ladder spilled from the side and dropped down just outside the window. Jaime climbed up into the cockpit, and Scott and Victor followed.

"Thank goodness you're all safe!" Orville Wright exclaimed. "I've been searching for you for hours."

"Dr. Franklin's down there!" Jaime yelled. "We can't just leave him!"

"I'll try to pull in closer," Orville said. He maneuvered the gyroplane lower until the ladder dangled just above Franklin.

Franklin looked up and roared. A zombie grabbed on to the rope ladder, but Franklin pulled him off and tossed him aside.

"Climb on, Ben!" Victor called.

Franklin waved the gyroplane away. Victor watched in horror as his friend was swallowed by the raging mob.

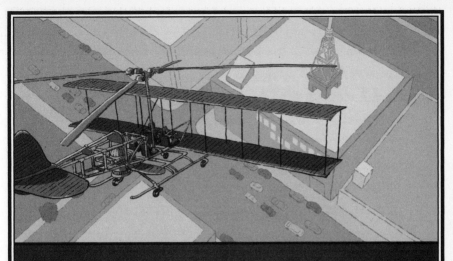

CHAPTER NINETEEN
Mission: Destruction!

Jaime sat in the front seat, explaining to Orville everything that had happened. Victor and Scott sat silently behind them.

Once again, Ben had sacrificed himself to save others. But this time, Victor feared, there was no saving him.

"Scott," Orville shouted over the sound of the engine, "I have some good news for you. While on patrol, my brother flew over WURP and rescued your father from the rooftop."

"Really?" Scott said. "He's okay?"

"Right as rain. He and Wilbur are patrolling the city, picking up anyone who hasn't fallen under the Emperor's spell. They've managed to save quite a few already."

Victor smiled. "That's the best news I've heard all day."

Under Orville's steady guidance, the plane cruised high over the city. Victor watched the terrifying scene below. Thousands of zombies formed long, perfect lines, loading cartons of lightbulbs into waiting trucks. Others marched in thick clusters down the streets like swarms of army ants.

"Isn't there anything we can do?" asked Scott.

"We're doing it," said Jaime. "Our job is to get to Infinity Unlimited as fast as we can and destroy the supertransmitter. There's the building up ahead."

As the gyroplane approached the factory, Victor could see thousands of zombies lined up at the back like trains at a freight yard. Half the lines were entering the building, and the other half were leaving, each zombie carrying a large box of lightbulbs. The lines were orderly and moved with steady precision.

"There's no one on the rooftop," said Orville. "I'll set down there." He pulled up on a stick and the gyroplane rocked back and descended gently onto the factory. At the center of the roof, Victor recognized the top of the supertransmitter sticking up like a radio tower.

"You sure you don't want me to wait?" asked Orville.

"There are people out there who need your help," said Jaime.

"I won't be far," said Orville. "Be careful, all of you." He revved the throttle and lifted up into the air. The gyroplane banked to the left and disappeared around a building.

"What now?" said Scott.

"We need to get to my parents," said Jaime. "If we can free them from Napoléon's control, they'll know how to stop the supertransmitter."

They ran over to a door. Jaime opened it a crack and peered inside. "The stairwell's empty. Once we're in, we'll need to move fast."

They took the stairs two at a time. At the bottom, they paused outside the red metal door to catch their breath.

"What's that sound?" whispered Scott.

"The power plant," said Jaime.

"But it's louder," said Victor. He gulped. "A *lot* louder."

Jaime turned to Victor. "Ready?"

"No, but here goes." He pushed open the door and stepped inside. It swung shut behind them. The room was just as it had been the last time. The supertransmitter's antenna stood tall on an island in the center of the room. The giant electrical turbine beneath spun furiously, so fast that Victor couldn't even see the whirring blades.

Jaime pointed to the center of the island. Her parents sat at a console at the base of the giant antenna, a vacant, hypnotized look on their faces. "There they are. Any ideas?"

"Try these," said Victor. He reached into his knapsack and pulled out two pairs of sunglasses. "If your parents wear these, it might weaken the connection between them and Napoléon."

"It's worth a shot," said Jaime. Scott stood watch at the end of the footbridge as she and Victor inched across to her parents. The first time they had crossed the bridge, the electrical energy had felt like a breeze on their skin. Now, with the blades beneath them spinning at full speed, it felt like a hurricane.

When they were right behind her parents, Jaime reached around and placed one pair of sunglasses over her mother's eyes. Victor placed the other pair on her father's.

"Mom, Dad—it's me, Jaime!" She shook them again. Slowly, they turned their heads to face her.

"Jai-me?" Jaime's mother's voice was deep and slow, as if she were waking from a long sleep. "What . . . Where are we?"

Jaime's father surveyed the room, taking everything in. "How did we get here?"

"There's no time to explain right now," said Jaime. "We need to shut down this supertransmitter. Can you do it?"

"Supertransmitter?" said her mother. It was as if she were seeing the enormous machine for the first time.

"Yes," said Jaime. "The Emperor is using it to control the entire city. You need to stop it!"

"How?" said her father.

"Try to focus," said Jaime. Victor could see she was struggling to remain calm. "You're electrical engineers. This is what you do."

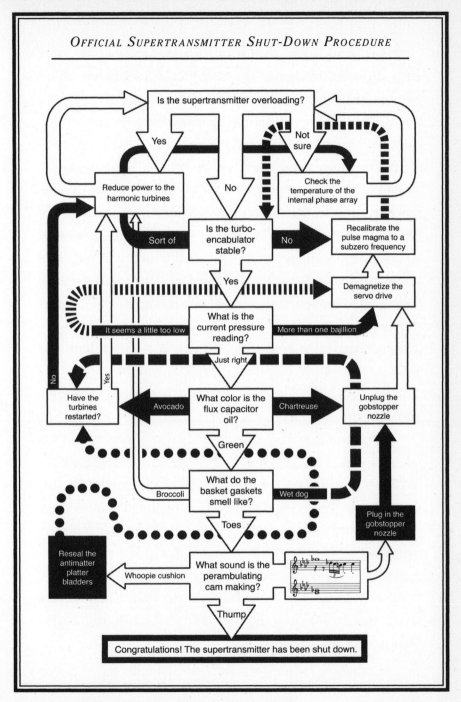

"It is?" said her mother thoughtfully.

"I do seem to remember something about that," said her father. "Let me think for a moment . . ."

"We don't have a moment," insisted Jaime.

"You most certainly do not!"

The voice was cold and forceful. Victor recognized it at once.

He turned to see the Emperor Napoléon sitting in his robotic bathtub at the far end of the room. Edison stood at his side, holding a hand over Scott's mouth. A long line of zombie scientists filed in from a door behind them. Trudging in unison, they circled the room. The island was surrounded.

Scott struggled free from Edison and ran across the bridge to meet up with the others at the center.

Napoléon and Edison strolled to the end of the bridge.

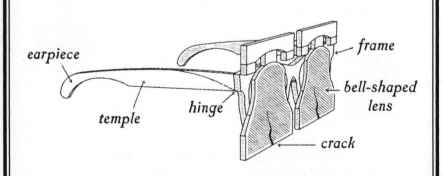

LIBERTY BELL SUNGLASSES

Benjamin Franklinstein Meets Thomas Deadison

"This will not do," Napoléon hissed. "My patience has worn thin."

"Mom, Dad!" pleaded Jaime. "You need to concentrate!"

"Ignore her," said Napoléon, speaking into his microphone. *"Mr. and Mrs. Winters, you will continue to operate the supertransmitter as instructed."*

Jaime's parents looked at each other, confused.

"Thomas, please remove those ridiculous glasses from the Winterses, then get rid of the children."

Edison took a step forward onto the bridge.

"Wait!" Scott shouted. "Your shoelaces! They're untied!"

Edison stopped and looked down at his shoes. "They aren't untied."

"Ignore him, Thomas," said Napoléon. "He's just trying to confuse you."

"I mean, your fly is open!" said Scott.

Victor knew Scott was stalling. But if they could hold off Napoléon for another minute, it might give Jaime's parents time to recover.

"Hold on," said Victor. "Don't you want to know why your hypnosis doesn't work on us?"

Napoléon smiled. "I do. And my plan was to study you later to discover the answer. But now I have a better plan."

Victor looked over at Jaime. Despite her efforts, Mr. and Mrs. Winters were still in a daze. "What plan?" he said.

"Why, to examine your bodies *after you're dead*!" said Napoléon with a laugh. "Thomas, kill them!"

CHAPTER TWENTY
Clash of the Monsters

CRASH!

The red door smashed off its hinges, knocking half a dozen zombies to the floor. Franklin stood in the doorway, his eyes blazing and his fists clenched. The metal bolts on his neck crackled with blue and white sparks.

"Rrrrrrraaaaaaaaggggrrrrr!"

"No!" Napoléon shrieked.

Franklin stormed into the room. Orville and Wilbur Wright rushed in after him. Skip followed behind.

"Scott," Skip yelled, "are you all right?"

Scott pointed at Napoléon. "He was going to kill us!"

Napoléon glared at the intruders. "Stop them!"

The zombies closed in on Franklin. Dozens of hands

clawed at him, reaching out to pull him down. Franklin flung them aside with ease.

Like a general commanding his troops, Napoléon sprang into action and began to issue orders. "Edison! Stop Dr. Franklin."

Edison charged toward Franklin.

Napoléon turned to his army of hypnotized scientists. "Prometheans—kill the children!"

Zombies rushed toward the bridge.

"We're trapped!" Scott shouted. "What do we do?"

"There's only one thing we can do," Jaime said, balling her hands into fists. "Fight or die!"

The zombies stampeded toward the bridge. Suddenly, as if from thin air, the Wright brothers appeared. They blocked the bridge entrance, shoving the zombies, clouting them on the ears, and confusing them with their harmonically charged superhuman speed.

"Hold them off for as long as you can!" Victor shouted. "We need to destroy the supertransmitter!"

Jaime turned back to her parents. "Mom, Dad—try to remember. You helped build this thing. How do we stop it?"

Mr. and Mrs. Winters examined the control panel. Gradually, they began punching buttons, flipping levers, and twisting dials.

"Is this right?" Mr. Winters asked.

"I don't know," Mrs. Winters said.

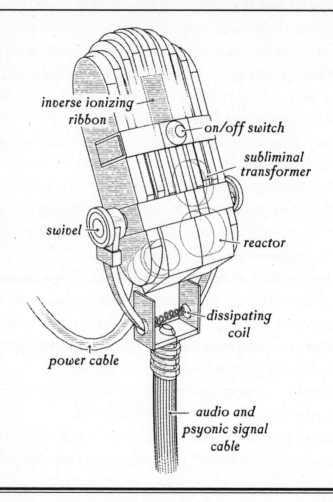

inverse ionizing ribbon

on/off switch

subliminal transformer

swivel

reactor

power cable

dissipating coil

audio and psyonic signal cable

"I know you can do it," Jaime said. "Just keep trying."

As Victor, Scott, and Jaime urged her parents on, a battle was being waged across the room.

Edison leapt at Franklin and knocked him to the ground. Skip Weaver jumped on Edison's back. "You're messing with the wrong meteorologist!" Skip said. "Meet the Weather Wrestler!"

He wrapped his arms around Edison and locked his fingers behind the old man's head. "Invent your way out of *this* move, smart guy!"

Edison shrugged and sent Skip skidding across the floor. He slid to a stop at the base of Napoléon's bathtub. Edison stood and charged at Skip, his face filled with fury.

"Behind you!" Napoléon warned.

Franklin sprang to his feet and launched himself at Edison. Edison staggered back. Franklin rushed at him again and drove him against Napoléon's bathtub, knocking it onto its side. Harmonic fluid spilled from the tub, and the microphone rolled away.

Napoléon tumbled onto the floor.

"Help!" he cried. "Protect your leader!"

Victor glanced at the withered little man, dressed in full military regalia from the waist up and soggy, silken bloomers from the waist down. Suddenly, the once-mighty Emperor seemed much less menacing.

A mob of zombies climbed onto Franklin's back, but he swatted them off.

Edison tore a pipe from the wall and swung it at Franklin's head. Franklin caught it in his hand. The two men grappled with each other as more zombies closed in.

Skip scrambled across the floor and picked up Napoléon's microphone.

"Put that down!" screamed Napoléon. "You don't understand its power!"

A funny look appeared on Skip's face. He switched on the microphone.

"Hi, everyone. This is Skip Weaver. You are not hypnotized anymore. I repeat, you are not hypnotized anymore. Also, be sure to catch my forecast every night on WURP."

The zombies stopped what they were doing. They looked around, confused.

"They're all free!" Scott hollered. "You did it, Dad!"

"Yeah," Skip said. "I guess I did!"

"Give me that!" screamed Napoléon.

"Why don't you get it yourself?" Skip threw the microphone down into the spinning turbine, where it was ground into dust and electrons.

"Nooooooo!" Napoléon howled, reaching his arm across the floor.

CLANG!

Edison hurled a chunk of steel at Franklin, who swatted it away.

"Raaaarrrrrghhhhhh!"

"Hey, why is Edison still hypnotized?" Scott asked.

"It's the supertransmitter," Victor said. "Until we can

stop it, the Emperor's connection with him can't be broken! Any luck, Mr. Winters?"

"Nothing's working." He studied the console with frustration. "I don't understand it."

Mrs. Winters gazed at the spinning turbine. "If we could somehow jam the blades . . ."

"Maybe we can," Victor said. "Ben! We need your help!"

Across the room, Franklin sent Edison flying into a wall. He turned toward Victor, his head cocked to one side.

"He doesn't recognize you," said Scott.

"It's me, Victor!"

"Vic-tor?"

"Ben, can you jam these blades with something?"

"Like the bathtub!" Scott shouted. "Throw it!"

Franklin lifted Napoléon's robotic bathtub high above his head. With a grunt, he hurled it down into the turbine.

It wedged itself between the whirring blades. There was a screeching, grinding sound, like a thousand fingernails dragging down a chalkboard. Sparks flew, and a horrible burning smell filled the air. The turbine trembled, its mighty blades held still by the metal bathtub.

"It worked!" Jaime exclaimed. "He did it!"

Franklin dropped to the floor, exhausted.

Edison blinked his eyes. "Where . . . where am I?"

The turbine creaked and groaned.

"Will it hold?" Jaime asked.

"I don't know," Mrs. Winters said, "but we may have a

bigger problem. According to these readouts, the dynamo is feeding back. It could go into meltdown."

"What does that mean?" Scott asked.

"If we can't bleed the extra energy," Mr. Winters said, "it will explode, taking half of the city with it."

Edison turned, a puzzled look on his face. "I did this, didn't I?"

"How do we stop it?" Mrs. Winters shouted.

Edison stumbled across the bridge and studied the control panel. "It's too late. You can't stop it," he said grimly. "But I can."

He climbed up to the second level and gripped two electrical terminals, one with each hand. His body stiffened as electricity coursed through his veins. He began to glow white.

"Thomas!" a weak voice called out. "I command you to stop! I am your Emperor!"

The inventor released his grip on the terminals. "My . . . Emperor?"

Crawling on his elbows, Napoléon dragged his withered body toward the footbridge. "Do not interfere. Let the dynamo explode."

"Don't be stupid!" Jaime shouted. "If it blows, you'll die too!"

He laughed a weary laugh. "With my Leyden casket destroyed, I cannot survive. And if I must die, so must you!"

CHAPTER TWENTY-ONE
All or Nothing

"Mr. Edison," Jaime cried, "please help us!"

"No, Thomas!" Napoléon demanded. "Return to me at once!"

"You don't . . . control me . . . anymore!" Edison grabbed the terminals again. White energy flowed into his hands.

Mr. Winters analyzed the readouts on the console. "It's working! Edison's absorbing the energy. But if the dynamo starts to spin again, we're done for."

CRACK!

"The bathtub!" Mrs. Winters cried. "It's not going to hold!"

With a horrifying crunch, the bathtub split in two and

was swallowed up into the turbine. Slowly, the great blades began to move again.

Equipment overloaded all around them, filling the room with sparks and smoke. Victor recoiled as a nearby generator exploded, showering him with sparks.

Edison glowed brighter and brighter. "Everyone, listen to me! I can't absorb any more electricity. You must leave or you'll be reduced to ashes!"

Around the room, the scientists were regaining their senses. Orville and Wilbur raced back and forth at superspeed, ushering them out the door to safety.

Jaime's parents continued to type frantically at the console, searching for any way to stop the turbines from spinning. "Jaime, you all need to go—now!" Mr. Winters ordered.

"But—"

"There's nothing you can do," Mrs. Winters said. "There's probably nothing we can do, either, but we need to try."

"We'll be right behind you," said Mr. Winters. "I promise. Now go!"

"Promise?"

"Promise."

Something snapped inside the great machine and it suddenly began to spin faster. Edison flashed like a camera. Jaime hugged her parents and ran for the exit.

Victor, Scott, and Skip raced to Franklin's side.

"Come on," Victor urged. "We need to leave right away!"

Franklin lurched for the door, then paused and looked toward the dynamo. Edison glowed white-hot as Jaime's parents worked desperately at the console. Franklin turned to Victor, confused.

"Why . . . do . . . they . . . ?"

"They're trying to stop the dynamo," explained Victor. "It's going to explode if they can't shut it down."

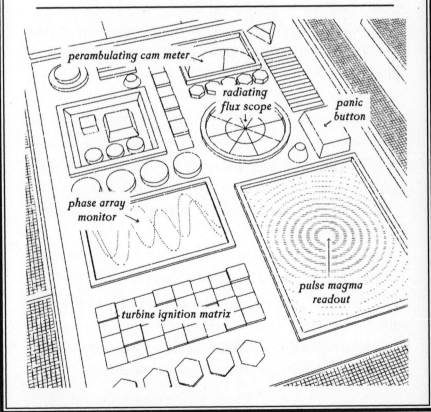

THE HARMONIC SUPERTRANSMITTER CONSOLE

perambulating cam meter

radiating flux scope

panic button

phase array monitor

pulse magma readout

turbine ignition matrix

"*I . . . can stop . . . dynamo!*" Franklin roared. "*GO!*" He pushed Victor, Skip, and Scott through the doorway. Victor watched as Franklin lumbered across the room, his finger pointing at the console where Jaime's parents sat. "*You! Go!*"

Mr. Winters looked up, an expression of confusion and terror on his face. "You don't understand. We need to—"

"*RAAAAAAAAAAAARGH!*" roared Franklin. He ripped the massive metal console from the floor and held it high above his head. Terrified, Mr. and Mrs. Winters scrambled across the footbridge and out the door.

Franklin carried the console to the end of the footbridge. Beneath him, the turbine was now spinning wildly out of control.

"I'm burning out!" Edison shouted. "Hurry!"

Franklin kicked the safety railing over and threw the console down into the turbine. It wedged itself between the blades and the machine came to a sudden stop. There was a horrible grinding noise and the floor began to quake.

Franklin leapt into the pit and began ripping the turbine blades from their axle.

Edison looked down at Franklin, his whole body aglow with electricity. "Yes! It's working! I'm absorbing all of it . . . all of it . . ." The air around him rippled from the intense heat.

At the doorway, Victor shielded his eyes from the brilliant light. The Wright brothers ushered the last of the scientists out. "That's everyone," Wilbur said. "Close the door."

"But what about Ben?"

An arm pulled Victor back and the door slammed shut.

There was a thunderous explosion, then all was silent and dark. The crowd of people filling the stairwell stood motionless.

"I'm going in!" said Victor. He threw open the door and raced inside.

A pungent burning smell filled the smoky air. Emergency lights flickered to life.

Victor looked up. Where Edison had once stood, there was now only a pile of smoldering ash. He raced to the pit. The turbine's steel blades had been torn off and twisted into useless strands. Franklin lay crumpled at the bottom of the pit, motionless. Steam rose from his jacket.

"Ben!" Victor climbed down a ladder to his friend and rolled him over. "Someone help!"

Jaime and her parents sprinted to Franklin's side, followed by Scott, Skip, and the Wright brothers.

Mr. and Mrs. Winters examined Franklin, checking his neck bolts for a charge and listening for a heartbeat.

"How is he?" Victor asked. "Is he going to be okay?"

Mrs. Winters looked up at him gravely. "He's dying."

Victor gasped. "No! Isn't there anything we can do?"

"We must return him to his Leyden casket at once," Mr. Winters said. "It's his only hope."

CHAPTER TWENTY-TWO
A Last Request

Victor pulled his bike up next to Scott's and paused to catch his breath.

"See, Victor? There's nothing like a good bike ride to clear your head. I try to clear my head at least once a day. Sometimes more."

Victor observed the city all around him. It was hard to believe that only a week earlier, everyone had been under Napoléon Bonaparte's hypnotic control. They didn't realize it, but they had Skip Weaver to thank. His message over the microphone hadn't just released all the scientists in the room. It had released *everyone* in the city.

"I just can't stop thinking about Ben," said Victor.

"Me too," said Scott. "But Jaime's parents haven't given

up on him yet. I mean, he's still alive . . . sort of."

Victor's phone beeped. He pulled it from his pocket and read the screen. "Something's happened."

Back at Victor's house, they ran into Orville and Wilbur, who had just arrived on their bicycles. Behind them, a WURP news van screeched to a stop on the sidewalk. Skip Weaver jumped out, dressed as an Italian sausage.

"I got the message," said Skip. "What's going on?"

"We don't know," said Wilbur.

The group raced into Franklin's apartment, then down the ladder to the secret laboratory. Jaime and her parents were standing over Franklin's Leyden casket.

"How is he?" Orville asked.

"He's waking up," whispered Jaime.

They gathered around the casket. Franklin's eyelids fluttered, then opened.

"Did . . . did it work?" His voice was weak. "Did we stop the Great Emergency? Did we stop the Emperor?"

Scott leaned in. "Napoléon's totally gone. He must have burned up in the explosion."

Franklin nodded. "And what of Edison?"

Wilbur shook his head. "He gave his own life to save the city."

"A noble sacrifice," said Franklin. His eyelids closed.

"Is he going to be okay?" Victor whispered.

Mr. and Mrs. Winters exchanged a sad look.

"No, Victor," said Franklin, opening his eyes again. "I am afraid this chapter of my life is drawing to a close."

"We can keep him in suspended animation in the Leyden casket," explained Mrs. Winters. "It's possible that someday we'll find a way to bring him back."

"Do not mourn," said Franklin, a faint smile upon his lips. "I have had the rare chance to live a second life, and the magnificent honor to spend it with all of you."

He motioned for Victor to step closer.

"Victor, you have done more for me than I can ever repay. But I have one final request."

Victor sniffled. "Anything."

"There is a box in my apartment, filled with gold. Enough to last you and your mother a lifetime. I want you to have it."

"I can't take your money, Ben."

"I'm not giving it to you. It will be payment for services rendered."

"I don't understand."

"I am about to begin another long sleep, and I will need special care. The care of someone I can trust with my life." He looked Victor in the eyes. "Will you be my Custodian?"

"Your Custodian?" Victor said. "But I don't know how to . . ."

Mrs. Winters put a hand on his shoulder. "We can help you."

1790–1832	George Whitlock
1832–1861	Zachary Whitlock
1861–1891	Abigail Whitlock Bowman
1891–1930	James Bowman
1930–1974	Edith Bowman Mercer
1974–1990	Clifford Mercer
1990–2011	Dean Mercer
2012–????	Victor Godwin

"We'll all help," added Skip.

Victor nodded, overcome with emotion. "I'd be honored, Ben."

"Mind you," Franklin said wryly, "this means you'll have to finally tell your mother about all this."

Victor smiled. "Of course."

Franklin began to wheeze. The Leyden casket emitted a series of beeps.

"It's time," Mr. Winters said. "We dare not wait any longer."

"Good-bye, Ben," Victor said. "I'll miss you."

"No, not good-bye," Franklin whispered. "Let us just say 'until we meet again.'"

Mr. Winters placed the breathing mask over Franklin's face, and the old man sank into the harmonic fluid.

Mrs. Winters closed the casket.

EPILOGUE

Victor sat on a hillside, reading a book. A kite string was tied to his foot.

"Hey, Victor."

"Oh, hi, Scott."

"What are you reading?"

Victor held up the book. "It's called *The Custodian's Guide to Maintaining Your Mop.*"

"That sounds boring."

"It's actually a secret guide to being a Promethean Custodian. There's a lot to the job I never knew about."

Scott sat down next to Victor. "So how's Ben doing? Any better?"

"Mostly the same. The Prometheans say his vital signs

are growing stronger. But it could be a long time before we can wake him up. Months, years . . . maybe even centuries."

Scott looked up. "Is that one of his kites?"

"Yup. He built it to study air currents." Victor squinted at the sky. "Are those storm clouds?"

"Can't be. My dad says one hundred percent clear skies all day."

"He does, huh?" Victor considered Skip's forecast and then began reeling in the kite.

"Hey, that reminds me," said Scott. "The science fair is in a couple of weeks. Want to team up on a project?"

"What are you thinking of?"

"Get this: a new potato battery . . . *made of eggplant!*"

"Eggplant?"

Scott's face fell. "What's wrong with eggplant?"

Victor laughed. "Nothing at all. It's exactly the kind of idea Ben would have loved." He stuffed the book into his backpack and threw the kite over his shoulder. "Let's get to work."

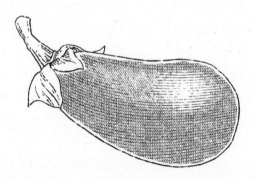

The rapid Progress true Science now makes, occasions my Regretting sometimes that I was born so soon. It is impossible to imagine the Height to which may be carried in a 1000 Years the Power of Man over Matter. We may perhaps learn to deprive large Masses of their Gravity & give them absolute Levity, for the sake of easy Transport. Agriculture may diminish its Labour & double its Produce. All Diseases may by sure means be prevented or cured, not excepting even that of Old Age, and our Lives lengthened at pleasure even beyond the antediluvian Standard. O that moral Science were in as fair a Way of Improvement, that Men would cease to be Wolves to one another, and that human Beings would at length learn what they now improperly call Humanity.

—Benjamin Franklin, 1780

© Christy McElligott

MATTHEW McELLIGOTT is the author of such books as *Even Aliens Need Snacks, Even Monsters Need Haircuts, The Lion's Share,* and the Benjamin Franklinstein series. A longtime member of the Fraternal Order of Zombies, he was recently appointed a Knight of the Living Dead.

www.mattmcelligott.com

LARRY TUXBURY has written over two books, including this one. When not writing, he teaches at the real Farnsworth Middle School outside Albany, New York, where he strives to become one of the brighter bulbs in the building. His teaching style is often described as "hypnotic" and his students follow him with an almost zombie-like passion.